THE DREAM
SQUAD

CAROLINE MACRORY

For Max and Mia

I hope that throughout your lives you'll have many wonderful and exciting adventures, both awake and asleep, and that you never stop dreaming.

Love you more than infinity.

MAGIC DREAMING

Think about this: we spend a third of our life sleeping and dreaming, yet we know very little about this part of our existence. Many people dismiss dreams as meaningless and insignificant. Some children even resist sleep and try to stay awake as long as possible.

Not me. I can't wait to climb into bed each night. Because, honestly, dreaming is one of the most exciting things you can do.

Dream lucidity is when you are asleep but you are aware that you are dreaming. That's the technical term, anyway. I prefer to call it 'magic dreaming' because I think that describes the experience better.

There's an awful lot that most people don't know about dreaming. I think it's fair to say that the more you discover about your dream world, the more exciting life becomes.

There are ways to enhance your dreams, such as drinking special herbal teas and keeping a dream journal. There are also techniques you can learn to make it easier to leave a dream (in other words, to wake up) or to stay in it for longer. I started to learn about all of this a few years ago when I began magic dreaming.

The big thing about magic dreaming is that it gives you a certain amount of control over your dream self…which means that if you practice and get good enough, you can decide where to go, what to do and who to spend time with in your dreams.

Magic dreaming is like any skill in some ways - the more you practice, the better you become.

The most important aspect of magic dreaming is that you have to believe. You have to believe in your abilities to master the dream world. If you believe, then you open your mind up to possibilities, and that is essential to explore fully another realm of existence.

So you see, there is a whole other dimension out there, waiting to be discovered, and trust me – it's a thousand times more thrilling than the 'awake' world could ever be.

So… what are you waiting for?

If you're not convinced, then read my story first and decide whether you're ready. It's about my first experiences of magic dreaming and how the Dream Squad was formed.

(P.S. I've put together a glossary on the next page, as I thought it might be helpful).

**Excerpt from The Dreaming Manual – written by
Jack O'Reilly, aged 12 years.**

GLOSSARY

Lucid Dreaming

Otherwise known as **Magic Dreaming**, lucid dreaming is when you are aware that you are dreaming. In a lucid dream, you can usually exert some control over the dream characters, the story and the environment. This can make dreaming pretty exciting!

Dream World or Dream Realm

The dream realm is both simple and complex. It is basically the world that you enter when you are asleep. Although it is separate from the 'awake' world, the two are entwined and impact on each other. The dream world is influenced by your subconscious. It can be a magical, exciting place to explore…and dangerous too.

Dream Signs

These are personal signs that recur in your dreams – themes that come up night after night. They can help you to know when you are dreaming because you learn to recognise the signs. Understanding your dream signs can also give you a window into your subconscious.

Dream Herbs

There are special teas and herbs that you can drink to encourage and enhance magic dreaming. There are also herbs that can set off nightmares.

Dream Maps

Dream Maps are used to assist magic dreamers to meet up together in their dreams. Usually Dream Maps outline the details of where and when you plan to go in your dream and any other details that may assist others to find you in the dream realm.

Anchor Object

Often included in Dream Maps (please see above), an anchor object is used to unite people in the dream world. By focusing on the same object, magic dreamers can - hopefully - meet up in the same dream.

Dream Trapping

This is an extremely rare and specialised act that involves trapping or locking someone in a dream or a nightmare so that they don't wake up in the 'real' world. It requires not only great power, but truly evil intent.

Dream Journals

A dream journal is a diary in which you record your dream experiences. This helps you to learn more about the Dream World and identify patterns in your dreams.

Dream Symbols

Sometimes you come across symbols in your dreams. An example of a Dream Symbol is a bird. Generally, birds are positive symbols. If you see birds in your dream, particularly doves, they symbolise your goals, aspirations and hopes for the future. However a bird with black feathers signifies death and decay. The black vulture is the most dangerous bird in the dream world. It symbolises evil and is a 'carrier' that spreads fear and nightmares.

CHAPTER ONE

J ack stood on the diving board, edging along it cautiously, gently bouncing up and down as it became springy under his bare feet. He could hear the distant sound of people laughing and splashing in the water far below him.

When he had gone as far as he could, he looked down. His toes were poking over the edge of the board. The pool was so far beneath him that his stomach did a somersault. He put his foot out, dangling it in the air as though he were going to find something solid there.

He looked down again, but now the pool had gone. All he could see were feathery wisps of cloud. The noises below had faded into silence.

He breathed in deeply and took a last look around. Was that the jagged tip of a mountaintop in the distance, jutting out above the clouds? The air felt cold and sharp, but he wasn't afraid. This was a familiar feeling and he knew what came next.

Closing his eyes, he flung out both his arms in front of him and jumped from the board. Instead of plunging downwards he hovered for a second before soaring forward into the wind. The cool breeze rushed into his face, tickling his nostrils and making his eyes water.

He was flying. And he had never felt so free.

Jack hovered and soared, dipped and dived, just as he imagined a bird of prey would do. A magnificent golden eagle. Or a red-tailed hawk, like the one he had seen with his mum at the wildlife park. Except that he didn't have a metal chain around his ankle like the hawk. Jack remembered feeling sad that this mighty bird could only fly from post to post. It must have longed to fly free - like Jack was doing now.

There was a beautiful sunset in the distance and the clouds felt soft to touch...in fact they felt a bit sticky, as if they were made of marshmallows. Jack had thought that clouds were made of marshmallows when he was younger. One day he had mentioned it to his older sister and she had laughed at him for being so silly. He felt a strange satisfaction now, because he could taste the sweetness.

Jack folded up his body in mid-air and did a somersault, before landing feet down on a little ledge that had appeared in the clouds. The ledge was attached to the side of a mountain, with a rugged path winding upwards.

Up a little way, and off to one side of the path, Jack could see a cave. He climbed up to it and saw that instead of being dark and bleak inside, as you might expect a of a cave, it was gleaming with bright colours that shone out from every wall. The floor of the cave was covered in a blanket of soft grass and summer flowers.

Jack stopped in his tracks. Despite knowing none of this was real, he could not believe what he was seeing. He rubbed his eyes, squeezed them shut and looked again.

There she was, right in front of him, as clear as day: Evie Sullivan.

Evie, who sat in front of him in his maths class at school. Evie, who was best friends with that annoying girl, Betsy, who was always interrupting the teacher to ask questions.

Evie stared back at him, a quizzical expression on her face, the same one she sometimes had when she was puzzling over a difficult maths question. She appeared to be just as confused as Jack.

And then, in a flash, Jack disappeared.

Chapter Two

J ack opened his eyes. He lay still, looking at the grey light of a winter dawn filter through the window. It took him a second or two to remember he was in his bedroom at home. He rolled over and nestled deeper into his bed covers, like a hibernating animal.

He thought about Evie. 'What on earth…?' he muttered to himself, but as he tried to work out what had just happened he was interrupted by an almighty yell.

'JACK!!!!'

Jack winced. What a way to wake up. It was the same every morning and it wasn't pleasant. He braced himself for the next part.

'JACK! You've got 10 minutes to get up and have breakfast before I boot you out of the door. I'm telling you now, if I get one more letter about you being late…I'll… I'll…'

Jack's mum, Elaine, never did get around to telling him what would happen if she got one more letter about him being late. Her voice trailed off, and he listened to her thumping around the kitchen and crashing mugs and plates on to the table as though she wouldn't be happy until they were all chipped and broken.

He wished he was still soaring above the mountaintops, discovering magical, colourful caves.

Jack dragged himself out of his warm nest. There was nothing worse than getting out of bed in the winter, when it was still murky outside. Those horrible cold moments between crawling out of bed and managing to throw enough layers of clothes on to create some warmth. Since mum had lost her job and dad had been demoted, money had been tight. Mum insisted that heating the house was a luxury to be saved for special occasions, like when there were guests round (which was rare these days).

Jack grabbed his clothes, pulling his trousers over one leg so quickly that he ended up hopping around trying to get in his other leg without losing his balance. He grabbed his t-shirt and jumper, ran his comb once through his hair and trudged down the hallway to the bathroom to brush his teeth.

He wasn't hungry, but his mum shoved a piece of buttered toast into his hand anyway as he ran down the hallway to the front door. He paused to grab his coat and school bag.

'Don't slam the --- !' he heard his mum shout as he slammed the door behind him. But he didn't hear her. All he was thinking was that he MUST find out about Evie.

CHAPTER THREE

J ack was a pupil at St Bartholomew's, which wasn't far from where
he lived. It was a brisk ten-minute walk up the road, but could take
him twenty minutes when he was dawdling. Sometimes he saw
Oliver and Sammy, the twins from the year above, and he walked with
them. The twins finished each other's sentences and bickered quite a lot
and usually wanted Jack to walk in between them. If Jack didn't see the
twins, he would occasionally knock for Jessica O'Brien, even though he
found her quite irritating. She had a high-pitched voice and all she ever
did was whine about things. She always seemed so pleased when Jack
called for her though, so sometimes he did it just to be kind.

Not today though. This morning Jack had a lot to think about, and
he was hoping for no distractions.

He waited until he was a safe distance from the house before lobbing
his soggy toast over the fence that separated the path from a row of
allotments. He aimed for the compost heap, but the toast bounced off a
scarecrow's head, the one that Mr Blake had put next to his strawberry
plants to stop the crows gorging on them in summer. There was frost
on the ground now, though, and there weren't any birds to scare. The
scarecrow looked a bit sad and obsolete, Jack thought.

It was a grey, drizzly morning in late November. The sun had
supposedly risen, but you could hardly tell as it was still so dreary.
Although Jack hated the cold, for once he barely noticed it as he trudged

up the road, his hands shoved deep into his pockets, staring at his feet, deep in thought.

All he could think was seeing Evie Sullivan in his dream. Evie Sullivan! What in the world had she been doing in that cave?

Jack didn't even know Evie that well and had never thought much about her. He supposed that she was quite pretty, now he came to think of it, but he would never have admitted that to anyone and he had certainly never spoken it out loud.

Evie usually sat in front of him in Mrs Murphy's maths class. Jack remembered he had once sat on the same table as her in the chemistry lab. They'd hardly spoken, although he remembered they'd had a giggle over Mr Burley's comb-over hairstyle. Mr Burley was their chemistry teacher. He was a kind, gentle and patient man. He adored the children and they felt the same way about him. He had a large bald patch that he tried to cover up in increasingly inventive ways. Sometimes he swept his hair over it, and other times he would wear a hat. On a couple of occasions he had come into class wearing a toupee. It wasn't the same colour as what was left of his real hair, and it looked so silly that the children had to smother their laughter. Evie had whispered to Jack that Mr Burley would do better to embrace the bald patch and be proud of it. Jack had chuckled. And that was it. Jack only remembered it because he had felt a little guilty at making fun of his favourite teacher. That was the extent of their communication, as far as he could recall. And that was weeks ago. So why on earth had she popped up in his dream?

Jack felt that it must mean something, but he had no idea what. And it wasn't as though he could just march right up to her and ask her about it.

Chapter Four

Ever since he'd started lucid dreaming, Jack had gone on countless adventures. He had swum along the bottom of the deepest oceans; crossed deserts; explored space; lived in medieval castles and visited futuristic lands where robots ruled the world. He had sailed the seven seas and discovered magical islands with talking animals and treasure troves. He had encountered wild creatures, extinct animals and mythical beasts.

Jack often flew in his dreams. This was a recurring theme for him. He had always longed to be able to soar through the clouds and now he could, so he chose to do that time and again while he slept. The feeling of total freedom was just as good – even better perhaps – than he had imagined it would be.

Sometimes Jack had nightmares, but these were rare. He was getting better at controlling his dreams and influencing what happened. But sometimes the evil creatures that lurked in the depths of his mind crept into his dreams, even though he tried to stop them.

If that happened, he tried to wake himself up. He was getting better at that. He'd discovered that yelling at the top of his lungs in his dream could startle him awake. He'd also found that if he pinched himself over and over again in his dream, he would end up pinching himself in real life and wake himself up. It wasn't always effective, but it had worked once or twice.

Last night, though, had been special. It was the first time he had seen someone he knew in a lucid dream. He used to dream about people when he was younger, of course, but since he had started magic dreaming, he had always gone exploring on his own.

He wondered what it meant. Was there any way Evie could have seen him too? It had certainly looked that way. No, of course not. That wasn't possible. It was HIS dream.

Mind you, he'd never talked to anyone else about his dreaming, apart from his Great Granny Georgia. That was partly because he didn't know how to explain it to anyone. Jack was a quiet boy. People mostly thought of him as sensible and ordinary. He generally liked to keep his head down and keep himself to himself. And he was pretty sure that if he did start talking about magic dreaming, people would think he'd gone completely mad.

But now it looked as if he might have to break that rule…

Chapter Five

J ack had started magic dreaming one night a few months earlier,
when he was staying with his Great Granny Georgia.

Jack loved going to stay with his great granny. She was old and
kind and gentle. He loved his parents, but his mum was loud and shouty
and always seemed to be nagging him or his sister, Bella. Bella was fifteen
and she was always staying out late and seeing her friends at the weekend
and she continually argued with their mum about what she was and
wasn't allowed to do. Sometimes their arguments gave Jack a headache
and he would retreat to his bedroom and put on his headphones or go
on his computer. Jack's Dad could be fun, but he worked long hours and
wasn't at home much. Since money had become tight, both his parents
seemed stressed more often than not.

So Jack loved going to stay with his Great Granny Georgia. It was
like a sanctuary for him. The house was musty and every room was full
of fascinating and unusual objects. Great Granny Georgia was a bit of
a hoarder. Mum and Dad used to mutter about all her stuff in critical
tones, complaining that one day they would be the ones who would have
to sort through all that junk.

Jack thought her house was wonderful, though. Especially the attic.
That was a true treasure trove. If the rest of the house was crowded, the
attic was something else altogether. It was piled high with objects that
Great Granny had collected over the years. There were old mannequins,

tiny china jugs, soft toys that had lost limbs and had their stuffing spilling out of them; there were piles and piles of old books and magazines, so ancient that their pages had crinkled up and the print had faded; there was an ancient dressing table, and a rocking horse with only one eye; there was a dressing table full of mouldy scarves that smelled terrible; there was a collection of pressed flowers and a drawer full of key rings. There was everything you could imagine. Jack could happily spend hours and hours in that attic, rummaging through the treasures.

The best part, though, was that Great Granny Georgia had a story to tell about each and every object. She found it hard to climb into the attic these days, with her stiff knees and aching back, but sometimes she would duck her head and make her way up the creaky ladder, just because she knew how much Jack loved it up there. Then they would sift through the objects together, and Jack would ask her for the story behind each one.

'The rocking horse... well now, let me see... that was given to my sister Nelly on her sixth birthday by our neighbours one Christmas. It was unusual to receive gifts like that in those days, but our neighbours were kind and rich and they didn't have children of their own, so they always gave us expensive presents. Nelly loved that rocking horse so much that one day she sat on it all day, from morning until bedtime. She said she was riding it all the way to Land's End. She refused to get off it even to eat...'

Jack would stare at the old, one-eyed horse and try to imagine it being loved that much.

Great Granny Georgia had a wonderful imagination. She would make Jack a special warm drink after supper, some sort of herbal tea, and as she tucked him into bed, she would tell him amazing tales of magical lands, unicorns and dragons.

One night, Jack asked her who had told her all these stories. He was trying to picture Great Granny Georgia as a little girl, tucked up in bed, being told stories by her own great granny. Great Granny Georgia leaned forward, so that Jack could feel her sweet, musty breath against his skin and her whiskers tickling his cheek.

'Why Jack, I've experienced all these adventures myself,' she whispered. 'Every night I go exploring in the dream world, even now in my old age. I am still young in my dreams, you see. Young and free.'

Then she lowered her voice so much that Jack only just caught the words. 'It runs in our blood, Jack. All you have to do is open your mind. Your dream world is just as real as the awake world.'

And with those words, she clicked off the bedside lamp. Jack listened to her shuffling across the creaking floorboards to the bedroom door and out on to the landing.

That night he had his first lucid dream.

It was a while before he properly understood what had happened, but he knew from the beginning that it was something special and that he had tapped into a new dimension of some kind. He also knew it was something he had to keep exploring.

All of a sudden, Jack couldn't wait to go to bed in the evenings. His mum and dad could hardly believe it as he had always hated bedtime and resisted going upstairs. They figured that Great Granny Georgia must be a good influence on him, and they started to send him there every fortnight, which was just fine with Jack.

CHAPTER SIX

Jack was still deep in thought as he trudged through the gates of St Bartholomew's that morning.

St Bartholomew's was a big school and there were plenty of other children plodding through the gates alongside him, all heading into the playground to wait for the first bell to ring. They reminded him of robots. Weary robots, all hunched over with their backpacks on their shoulders, staring at the ground just like he was. It was strange how so many of the children seemed to be worn out all the time lately.

Jack checked the timetable in his homework journal and saw that he had history with Miss Spangle first period, followed by English with Mr Solomon. After morning break, it was French with Madame Bovaire and in the afternoon he had double chemistry with Mr Burley. He remembered that he hadn't finished his chemistry homework and he vaguely wondered if Mr Burley would notice or mind. He was the most supportive teacher in the school so Jack thought he would probably let him off.

Jack couldn't concentrate on school work, though. He kept wondering if Evie could have known she was in his dream. Seeing her in the cave had been so vivid. It had felt just as real as the other parts of his dream – almost as real as if he had seen her in the classroom on a normal day. But, no, surely it couldn't be possible for two people to be in the same dream…could it?

As he walked into the classroom, he looked round for Evie, trying not to be too obvious. He spotted her in the far corner, sitting with her best friend, Betsy. Evie glanced up at the same time and their eyes locked. A look passed between them.

She knows! Jack felt sure of it.

Both of them looked away, embarrassed.

Jack decided to be brave and he made his way over to where the two girls were sitting. 'Did you, um, I was just wondering if you…well, if you wanted to talk about last night?'

Betsy looked up sharply, and Evie's cheeks went red.

'What's he talking about?' demanded Betsy.

Evie ignored her. 'Okay…yeah, okay,' she faltered. Then she seemed to become more decisive. 'Betsy and I will be at the reading tree during morning break. We'll meet you there.'

Jack nodded. He was excited by the thought of discussing his dream with her, although he was disappointed that Betsy would be coming along too.

Betsy was very strong-willed and determined. Confident too. Sometimes she could be downright bossy. She was also extremely clever. Her mind was always working overtime, furiously trying to figure out the answers to life's mysteries.

Some of the other kids poked fun at her and called her a nerd and a bookworm, but she didn't seem to notice or care. She wore thick black glasses and her brown hair was scraped back into a slightly greasy ponytail. Betsy wasn't bothered about how she looked. 'Books not looks' was her motto. She always had her nose burrowed in one, whether it was on the bus to school, at lunch time, or even when she was walking down the street. Not fiction books either. She said those were mostly a waste of time.

Betsy wasn't great in social situations. She could be loud and domineering and she usually forgot to ask how people were or what they had been up to. Sometimes she'd interrupt rudely because she was so keen to get her point across. Jack couldn't help feeling that Evie had made an odd choice in picking Betsy for a best friend.

Break time arrived and Jack surveyed the classroom. If Evie was going to bring a friend to the reading tree, he would too. His eyes settled on Mouse. Yes, Mouse was a good choice.

Mouse wasn't his real name, of course, but he'd been called Mouse for as long as anyone could remember. Even the teachers and his dad called him Mouse. Hardly anyone could remember his real name.

Mouse was called Mouse because he had a habit of wrinkling up his nose ...just like a mouse. He did it a lot – whenever he was excited or nervous or worried about something, or even if he was just thinking hard. Sometimes he rubbed his ear at the same time, which somehow made him look even more like a mouse. So the name stuck.

Mouse was smaller than the other kids in the class and he was quite different to the rest of the boys. He didn't like playing football or running around outside, and he was quite shy. He was quiet and thoughtful and he was a loyal friend. You could rely on Mouse to be true to his word.

Years ago, Mouse's mum had died. It had happened before Jack knew him. Jack's mum said she'd heard that Mouse's mum had died of an illness when he was about six. It had been just Mouse and his dad for a good while now.

Jack trusted Mouse and was confident he wouldn't think this whole dreaming thing was crazy. Yes, he was definitely the right person to bring along for moral support. He sidled up to him and said in a hushed voice: 'I… well, how do I put this? I have to go to a… a secret meeting. I need… I need a…' he struggled to think of the right term… 'I need a spokesperson.' He was not entirely sure what the word meant or even what he was asking Mouse to do.

Mouse wrinkled up his nose and rubbed his ear. He didn't seem sure.

'I promise it won't be boring,' said Jack. 'It will be the strangest thing you've ever heard.'

Mouse shrugged 'okay' and followed Jack to the reading tree.

CHAPTER SEVEN

nd that's how The Dream Squad was formed.

The four of them – Jack, Evie, Betsy and Mouse - gathered that morning for what would turn out to be the first of many Dream Meetings over the coming months. When they were at school, they always met at the reading tree - a big old weeping willow. Tucked away behind the curtain created by its branches, they felt safe to discuss and explore their dream secrets.

That first morning, Jack and Evie established that they had indeed been in the same dream. Evie went first. 'For as long as I can remember, I've always had vivid dreams. But lately, it's funny... because I've started choosing where I go and what happens. I know that I'm asleep and I know that it's all a dream, and I can sort of … make things happen.'

She looked around at her audience, trying to gauge whether they believed her or not. Satisfied that they did, she went on: 'Last night, I went to a wonderful fairground. There were amazing rides and stalls with free candy-floss and giant lollipops as big and round as basketballs. Then I hopped onto a rollercoaster that wasn't attached to any kind of track. It just soared into the air and whizzed around the clouds, stopping every now and again so that I could jump out and roll around in the fluff. Then I wanted to go somewhere a bit quieter, so the rollercoaster pulled up on a mountainside. I hopped out and saw these beautiful caves. They were calm and peaceful and had wonderful colours shining out of them. There was the softest grass and a carpet of flowers. I went into the nearest cave and was staring at the beautiful array of colours when I heard a noise. I turned around…and that's when I saw Jack.'

Jack's eyes widened. 'That's where I found you,' he murmured. 'In the colourful cave on the mountainside. I had been in a different dream though. I had been flying… soaring through the air, doing somersaults, higher than any bird. And there was a little ledge on a mountain that was poking through the clouds. Something made me stop off there and that's when I saw the cave… that's when I saw you.'

Betsy looked from one to the other. 'So what happened then? Did you speak?'

'I woke up at that point,' said Jack. 'Seeing Evie was the last thing that happened.'

'So…' pondered Mouse, 'your dreams overlapped. You were having different dreams and somehow they became entwined. You could say your dream worlds collided.'

'But that's impossible!' declared Betsy. 'A dream is personal. It is part of your subconscious. It's not like another dimension where you can go with other people.'

As they were thinking about this, their meeting was interrupted by an almighty bellow.

'EVERYONE INSIDE IN FIFTEEN SECONDS OR IT'LL BE DETENTION FOR A MONTH!'

They scrambled from beneath the branches of the tree and ran to the classroom door before their headmistress, Miss Longbottom, could dole out her threatened punishment.

CHAPTER EIGHT

Miss Longbottom was not a pleasant woman. In fact, she was downright vile. Her name was Longbottom, which was funny, because in fact she had a very wide bottom rather than a long one. All of her was wide. She looked as if she had been flattened by a giant rolling pin. She walked with a funny waddle and no one had ever seen her smile.

Miss Longbottom loved punishing children and set herself goals to punish as many as possible each day. The detention room was always full at St Bartholomew's. Word had it that she had a flip chart in her office and awarded herself a gold star for every punishment she doled out.

You didn't even need to do anything bad to be punished by Miss Longbottom. Sometimes she meted out multiple detentions or confiscated lunches just because a child looked at her in a certain way. One time she made Mouse stand in the corner of the assembly hall for a whole morning because, she said, he had scrunched up his nose at her. She apparently didn't know that he did this all the time, to everyone, and that he didn't mean any offence by it. Or maybe she did know but didn't care.

Miss Longbottom had a number of eccentricities. Perhaps the most peculiar was that she kept a bird in her office. No one had ever seen the bird – not even a glimpse. It was kept in a cage that was covered with a black cloth. But any poor child who was unlucky enough to have been summoned into her office reported back that that you could see the shape of the birdcage under the cloth and you could hear a raspy, hissing sound coming from it.

And sometimes Miss Longbottom would have a jet-black feather sticking to her clothes...

Jack had often wondered what type of bird it was. But no one had ever dared to ask Miss Longbottom. There was a tale that someone had once plucked up the courage to ask if they could see the bird and they had been put in detention for three years. It could have just been a made-up story, but no one was willing to take the chance.

Jack often wondered why someone who despised children as much as Miss Longbottom had became a head teacher in the first place. Why pick a job where you are continually exposed to the objects of your loathing? It was as though she had decided that her sole purpose in life was to punish children and make them suffer.

And another thing: how did Miss Longbottom get away with being so horrible? Well, she happened to be incredibly good at convincing the parents that she was acting in the best interests of their kids. She could be very plausible, and was able to swallow the revulsion she felt for the children when talking to their mums and dads.

Parents believed her when she shook her head sadly and informed them that their little Freddie or their little Amy was becoming unruly and disrespectful, and that she'd had to put them in detention for the entire week. 'Tough love,' she explained to them with a pained look. 'It's the best way, trust me. I've worked with countless difficult children and I've always got them back on the straight and narrow.' The parents, terrified that their children were becoming out of control, put their faith in Miss

Longbottom. She was a head teacher, after all. It stood to reason that she knew what she was doing.

Besides, the St Bartholomew's children knew better than to tell their parents what went on at school. They knew it was unlikely they'd be believed (most parents think that children exaggerate and complain in equal measure). And anyway, Miss Longbottom always found out if a child had blabbed to their parents, and for those children, well… let's just say things didn't turn out well.

That day, as the children rushed into their classroom, they wondered fearfully what kind of mood Miss Longbottom was in. Not that she was ever in a good mood, but some days were worse than others. If she was in a particularly foul mood, it wouldn't matter what they did. Even if they made it inside in fifteen seconds or under, she would find a way to punish them anyway.

She stood at the door, staring at the children in disgust as they hurried past. They kept their heads down, desperately trying not to catch her eye. Jack first, then Evie, then Betsy. As Mouse reached the door, Miss Longbottom checked that no other teachers were looking and stuck her foot out. Mouse went crashing to the ground, and Jack turned to see him cowering on the floor with Miss Longbottom looming over him.

Jack knew better than to intervene. There was no point in them both getting punished. As he sat down at his desk he heard Miss Longbottom's booming voice roar 'DETENTION' in poor Mouse's ear.

CHAPTER NINE

The next morning, as Jack walked through the school gates, Betsy sidled up to him and grabbed his arm.

'Lucid dreaming,' she whispered in his ear.

'Huh?'

'Get the others and let's all meet at the reading tree at morning break. I have a LOT to tell you.'

Although he still found Betsy rather annoying, Jack couldn't help being intrigued. What had she discovered, he wondered? He struggled to focus in class that morning and kept staring at the clock. It appeared to be grinding to a halt. Time had a funny way of doing that – slowing down whenever you wanted it to go faster. Jack's parents always said that the older you became, the quicker time went past. Well, if that was true, right now he'd like to be older. A lot older.

At last it was morning break and the Dream Squad gathered under the branches of the reading tree. Betsy paused for effect, but she was clearly bursting to talk. 'Last night, I did a lot of reading about dreaming. And guess what…I found out all about these dreams you've been having. It's called Lucid Dreaming. Here, listen to this.' She opened the book and read from one of the pages:

Lucid dreaming (also known as magic dreaming) is the ability to recognise that you are dreaming while you are in the dream state. Once you are able to recognise that you are in a dream, you can gain greater control and even make conscious decisions in your dreams.'

Betsy looked up at the others to see their reactions. They watched her intently and waited for her to continue.

'There's a load more about it. It says people have been doing it for centuries and using their dreams for different things. Oh and this is interesting - it says children are more likely than adults to be "open" to the powers of lucid dreaming.'

This reminded Jack of something. 'I remember my Great Granny Georgia saying exactly that,' he said. 'Children are more susceptive to the dream world because their minds are more open to new experiences and possibilities in general...'

Evie looked thoughtful. 'So you're saying that this... this "lucid" dreaming... that it's actually a thing?'

'Yes! Listen... *Aristotle, a philosopher in ancient Greece, even talked about being conscious and aware within your dreams. People have been exploring their dream worlds since the beginning of time ...'*

'It's like an ancient secret,' murmured Jack. 'A secret that no one talks about.'

'Exactly', said Betsy. 'Except we're talking about it now. And I want to do it. You guys have to teach me how! I want to experience it too.'

CHAPTER TEN

The four children set about learning to dream. Or, to be precise, learning to dream magically. They'd always dreamed, of course. They'd had plenty of those dreams that faded away as you woke in the morning; ones that were vaguely interesting but were forgotten by breakfast. Now, however, they started to practice having extraordinary dreams. Magical dreams.

Jack was their guide. He was already good at it, and Great Granny Georgia had given him lots of tips. He shared these with the others. 'She told me to try meditating before I go to sleep. You close your eyes, breathe deeply and focus on where you want to go. It also helps to keep a Dream Journal. You should also keep repeating a mantra like "I will be aware that I am dreaming" as you fall asleep.'

Betsy, meanwhile, devoured books on lucid dreaming and told the others about tried and tested ways to enhance the dream world. 'I've found an entire book about dream herbs!' she told them one morning. 'There are teas and herbs that you can drink to help you to stay aware in your dreams.'

Jack frowned. 'What are these herbs exactly? Are they going to make us, you know, see things that aren't there?'

'Hallucinate you mean? No, I don't think so. They're all legal. Apparently, they've been used for centuries to help people have more vivid dreams.'

The others looked to Jack for approval. 'Well, I guess there's no harm in trying them', he said. 'It's just like drinking a herbal tea before bed, isn't it?' A thought occurred to him. 'Wait. The strange herbal tea my Great Granny Georgia gives me – I bet it's one of these special herbs – it must be! I always dream so much better when I'm staying with her.'

Mouse rubbed his ear thoughtfully. 'Wow… it's like a whole other world out there, the dream world. I mean, we're asleep for so much of our lives, aren't we? Why don't people talk about dreams more?'

Every day they met in their secret hiding place. Betsy usually brought the latest book she had found in the library and talked to them about ways they could become better at dreaming. They also started to recognise their own recurring dream signs – the themes that came up night after night.

Jack's personal dream sign was flying. He had known this for some time now. Whenever he found himself soaring through the air or hovering on the edge of a mountain ledge, he instantly knew he was dreaming.

Evie's dream sign was water. Usually she found herself swimming in her dreams. The moment she realised she was able to breathe under water was when she became aware she was dreaming. After that she'd had all kinds of aquatic adventures. Two nights ago she'd won an Olympic gold medal in the Women's Freestyle event. The night before that she had swum to a depth of twenty metres in the ocean and found a chest full of treasure in a sunken ship.

Betsy's dreams often involved a discovery of some sort – they were usually about science or space, sometimes history. She loved going back in time. Once she had gone back to the Roman occupation of Britain and helped some soldiers build Hadrian's Wall.

Mouse's dreams were quite different. They were fantastical and nearly always involved familiar storylines and characters from fairytales - magical quests, enchanted kingdoms and happy-ever-afters.

CHAPTER ELEVEN

They began keeping dream journals - a notebook next to their beds, in which they wrote down their dreams in as much detail as possible as soon as they woke up.

Sometimes Jack would wake in the middle of the night, forcing open his eyelids so that he could scribble down as much of the dream as possible before sinking back into sleep.

Other nights he dreamed all the way through to his morning alarm. Then he would grab his dream journal and write down everything he could remember before the details seeped away like grains of sand being washed away by the tide. Magic dreams tended to be easier to recall than regular dreams, but you could still lose some of the details if you didn't jot them down straight away.

The four of them would then bring their journals to school and read excerpts out to each under the reading tree.

Here are some of the entries written by the Dream Squad in the first few months of their dream exploration:

Jack – 11ᵗʰ November 2016

Last night I went flying again, but this time I flew alongside a plane. I could see the passengers sitting at the windows of the plane, but they couldn't see me. They weren't people I knew; they just had blank faces. I could see all the detail inside the plane, even what was playing on the TV screens. Then I dropped down on to one of the wings, and rode it like a surfboard.

Mouse – 16th November 2016

I've been having a series of circus dreams. Last night I was an acrobat in a stripy theatre. I was swinging on the trapeze and diving through rings of fire. I was juggling six knives at a time. I wasn't scared at all and I knew that I could do any act I attempted. Everyone I knew was in the audience. At the end they went wild, cheering and clapping. It was the best feeling in the world. I was wearing a wonderful outfit. It had bells and tassels that made music as I moved.

Betsy – 21st November 2016

I went into space last night in a rocket. I steered my spaceship round some of the better-known planets. I whizzed down Saturn's rings as though they were a giant slide. I went further into the universe and saw galaxies all around me. They were incredibly bright and were different shapes. Some looked like Catherine wheels. Others were like giant whirlpools.

Evie – 26th November 2016

I danced last night, beautiful elegant dancing. I was wearing a stunning dress made of sequins and feathers. After a while I looked down and saw that I was dancing on water. The water held my weight as though it was solid; it was a little springy and propelled me off the surface as I twirled around. I could see tropical fish below me as I danced, and beautiful anemones that seemed to sway in time with the music.

Jack – 12th December 2016

Not a great dream. I found myself in a desert. It was humid and stuffy and there were strange creatures roaming around. They were neither friendly nor threatening. They walked around like humans, on two legs, but they had the heads of wild beasts. I decided I wanted to leave this place so I tried to fly away, but I wasn't wearing my wings.

CHAPTER TWELVE

One day Betsy came up with an idea.

'I want to find you guys in my dream.' She turned to Jack. 'Like you found Evie in the cave that time. There must be a way to do it. They say that if you practice dreaming for long enough you can choose who you want to be with you in your dream.'

'So how do you do it?' asked Jack. 'Actually, I hardly ever have other people in my dreams. And if they do turn up, it's been unexpected… not necessarily because I've been thinking about them.' He looked at Evie, and she blushed.

'Well,' said Evie, 'it says in one my books that you have to wait until you are lucid dreaming and then simply imagine that they're there with you. If that doesn't work, you can try to visit the place you would normally see them in real life, and with any luck they'll be there. Or another way is to use an anchor object.'

'An anchor object?' asked Mouse.

'Yes – it's like an object you can all focus on together. It helps brings you to the same place.'

They pondered this for a few moments.

'Well, I suppose it makes sense in a way,' said Jack. 'I mean, we have a certain amount of control over what we do and what we see in our dreams, don't we? So why don't we all try to think of the same object and aim to go to the same place in our dreams and see if we can meet there…?' Jack trailed off and scratched his head. It sounded a little crazy saying it out loud.

'What about a sledge?' Betsy volunteered. 'My dad dusted off the one at home last night because it's forecast to snow at the weekend.'

'So we all focus on sledging in our dream?' suggested Jack, sounding hesitant.

'I guess it's worth a shot,' replied Betsy.

'We should organise a sleepover,' Evie said. 'Then we can all go to sleep at the same time and we can try going to the same place. Somewhere we all know well would be best I suppose. If we think really hard about where we want to go as we fall asleep we may be able to coordinate our dreams.'

'Yes, let's do it!' agreed Mouse.

'So where?' asked Betsy.

The school bell rang out shrilly, vibrating in their ears. They knew it wouldn't be long before Miss Longbottom's piercing voice echoed around the playground, sending everyone running for the classrooms.

'My place,' said Jack quickly. 'I'll sort it with my mum and dad.'

The others nodded and headed back to class, their heads full of the adventures they hoped lay ahead.

CHAPTER THIRTEEN

Jack planned the sleepover for the following Friday. He could hardly believe that his mum had agreed to it, but she had, on condition that they were all silent after 10 pm. If they weren't, she would get one of her migraines, apparently.

That was fine, Jack assured her, thinking to himself that they would all be fast asleep and dreaming by then anyway. They had no interest in staying awake.

Jack could barely contain his excitement on the day. This felt like a proper quest. Would they really all be able go on an adventure in the dream world? It felt as though they were on the brink of discovering something huge.

Jack's mum let him put out the sofa cushions and the spare mattresses in the living room so that they could sleep there together. They all brought their dream journals and Jack made them some dream herb tea, which they sipped while talking about the night ahead and discussing how they would find each other.

At one point Jack's sister, Bella, stomped through the living room on her way up to her bedroom. 'Why are you all drinking herbal tea, you freaks?' she muttered as she walked past. No one paid her any attention.

They were all snuggled inside their sleeping bags by 8 pm, but it took them longer to fall asleep than usual because they were so excited. It didn't help that Mouse kept sitting up every five minutes and asking whether anyone was still awake. Sleep seemed to be staying firmly on the other side of the room.

At last even Mouse was quiet. They had agreed to try and find each other in their usual place under a weeping willow tree in their dreams.

Jack was the first to fall into a deep sleep.

CHAPTER FOURTEEN

J ack was standing on a glacier. The sun bounced off the ice, glinting off the
surfaces and making rainbow icicles. He could feel its warmth on his face. He
looked down and found himself dressed in a snug all-in-one suit that felt furry
on the inside. He didn't feel cold at all.

He looked around, willing the others to appear. The landscape stretched out
before him, frozen and still, with no sign of life.

It was a strange place to find himself and Jack wasn't sure why he'd ended up
here. They had been learning about glaciers earlier that week in geography. Perhaps it
was linked? Or maybe it was connected to their anchor object, the sledge, that they were
all supposed to be focusing on. Except here was Jack, on a glacier, without a sledge or
any other kind of anchor object, without a weeping willow tree in sight and all alone.
Things weren't exactly going according to plan.

He focused on his friends' faces, whispering under his breath: 'Come on Evie and
Betsy. Come on Mouse. Come and find me.'

He trudged around, leaving footsteps in the ice, which was turning slushy. He
imagined a mug of hot chocolate, topped with marshmallows and whipped cream. A
second later, a steaming mug of chocolate appeared in his hands. It was exactly as he
had imagined it, right down to the marshmallows and whipped cream. He took a sip.
Hot chocolate had never tasted better.

Right - back to the mission. He called his friends' names again, his voice echoing
and bouncing off the glacier's icy towers. The snow was falling thick and fast now,
covering his footprints. Everything was white. His progress was slow and cumbersome

and he didn't know in which direction he should be heading. 'This is just a dream,' he said to himself. 'I am in control.'

He tried to imagine the sun shining, and as if by magic the snow began to melt and the ground felt firmer. Ahead of him a giant snowman melted into a puddle of water and a carrot. He felt a pang of sorrow, even though he knew it was a dream. His mum had told him that when he was little he used to cry when the snowmen he'd made shrivelled to nothing. 'But where have they gone?' he used to wail.

Jack found himself at the top of a great hill. He leant over the edge and looked down, wondering if he was going to fly again. In the distance, he saw something moving. It seemed to be growing bigger. He looked closer…yes, it was hurtling towards him. What on earth was it? Only when it was nearly upon him did he realise it was a sledge. A sledge whizzing along the icy snow. And on the sledge, whooping with glee, was Mouse!

'Wooooo hooooooo!! Weeee heeeeeee!!! Wooppeeeeee!!!'

'Mouse! It's really you. You're actually in my dr —'

Jack didn't get a chance to finish his sentence. The sledge hurtled into him, sending both of them flying. They landed in a heap and lay on the ice laughing.

'I can't believe it,' gasped Jack. 'You really are in my dream.'

'No, you're in MY dream,' replied Mouse, crinkling up his nose.

CHAPTER FIFTEEN

When they had caught their breath, they looked around. 'Any sign of the girls?' asked Jack.

'You're the only person I've seen,' said Mouse.

'Well, I guess we should look for them. We need to find the weeping willow tree. That's what we said we'd look for'.

'Well I don't recognise this place at all. One thing's for sure - it's not the school playground'.

'Maybe it doesn't have to be that particular willow tree. Let's just focus on seeing any tree. Picture it in your head, as clearly as you can…Betsy and Evie sitting under the tree.'

Mouse squeezed his eyes shut and tried to visualise the tree. When he opened them again, Jack was pointing at something on the horizon.

'Do you see what I see? It's the silhouette of a tree, with big hanging branches.'

'It's going to take ages to reach,' said Mouse.

'Well luckily we're in a dream. Oh — and we have our own transport!' They jumped on their sledges, which immediately began hurtling across the glacier like roller coasters on wheels. When they reached the tree, they parted the thick, drooping branches as though they were curtains and headed inside. Soon they arrived at a large clearing where the snow-covered ground had been replaced by a thick carpet of soft grass. Bars of sunlight streamed through the gaps in the branches and bright flowers were dotted across the ground. Evie and Betsy were sitting cross-legged, talking and laughing exactly as they would be in the real world. Except that they were dressed *in brightly coloured snowsuits and red bobble hats and their sledges were leaning up against the tree trunk.*

Betsy looked up, beaming. 'What took you so long?

Jack and Mouse sat down with them, thrilled to have found them. Jack lay on his back and stared up at the rippling patterns of the sunlight and branches above him. He closed his eyes. 'I am in a dream,' he murmured to himself. 'I am in a dream with my friends and we can do anything we want'. A wave of excitement washed over him and when he opened his eyes they were still sitting in a forest clearing, surrounded by brightly coloured trees and flowers. A stream of clear water trickled nearby. The sounds of birdsong and splashing water filled the air. Jack felt that the setting was vaguely familiar, as though it was from some happy distant childhood memory long ago.

'I'm hungry,' announced Betsy.

'That's funny,' said Mouse. 'I've never really thought about food in my dreams before. I don't think I've ever felt hungry. Or thirsty.'

Jack looked at him, surprised. 'Oh I have. In fact I've just had a hot chocolate with cream and marshmallows. I often dream about feasts. I'm going to imagine one now.'

Seconds later mounds of strawberries, cakes, sandwiches and biscuits appeared before them as far as the eye could see.

'The only food I ever really dream about is ice cream,' murmured Evie, staring intently ahead of her.

At that moment a river of vanilla ice cream began churning its way towards her. Creamy, thick, sweet ice cream. Mouse was amazed. He ran to the river and scooped up some into his mouth. 'I can taste it!' he exclaimed. 'Normally this would give me brain freeze!'

Evie laughed. 'Not in a dream. And you never get full either!'

'Or fat!' chuckled Betsy.

They all set about enjoying the picnic. They were having such a good time that at first they didn't notice the change in atmosphere or see the clouds above them start to grow black. A low growl filled the air, causing Evie to shudder and the others to look up in surprise.

'What was that?' whispered Mouse.

'I don't know…' said Jack nervously. 'Is someone having scary thoughts?'

'Not me', said Mouse. 'I was having happy thoughts. I was thinking about all this delicious food.'

Another growl echoed around the clearing and a shadow passed behind the tree beside them. Jack thought he heard the sound of gnashing teeth. 'Everyone focus on having only happy thoughts!' he hissed.

'I want to wake up now,' said Betsy, her voice starting to waver.

'How do we wake up?' asked Mouse.

'I'm not sure,' said Jack. 'If I'm desperate to leave a dream I usually I shout myself awake or pinch myself hard. Sometimes it works and sometimes it doesn't. It just depends how deeply I'm asleep.'

The shadows were drawing closer and the growling was becoming louder. A flash of lightning revealed that they were being circled by huge black creatures. Evie screamed. 'HELP! GET ME OUT OF HERE!'

'Whoever wakes up first, wake the others,' shouted Jack.

There was a flash of lightning and Mouse was gone.

The snarls became louder and the black creatures came closer. Their teeth were flashes of white in the darkness. Jack could feel hot breath on his face. It stank of rotten seaweed. 'Where's Mouse?' he shouted desperately. He had no idea if Mouse had managed to leave the dream or if he had he been dragged into the forest by one of the creatures.

He looked frantically for the others but he couldn't see them anywhere. As his eyes strained into the darkness he heard someone calling out his name, over and over, louder and louder.

'Jack! Jack! JACK!'

CHAPTER SIXTEEN

'Jack! Jack! Jack!'

His name was being repeated over and over again in a very loud and annoying voice. He opened his eyes a fraction.

He was back in the living room, and the faint light of early morning was coming through the window.

'Jack, what on earth is going on? Why are you all making such a dreadful racket? You've been yelling as if you were being dragged from your beds by kidnappers. And here's me having to be up for work in a few hours. I suppose you've been playing some silly game. Well, let me tell you, let me tell you this…'

She droned on and on while Jack tried to clear his mind and focus on what had happened. The glacier…the hot chocolates…the sledge…it had worked! They had found each other in their sleep!

Then he remembered the last part of the dream, the dark clearing, the terrifying creatures bearing down on them. He jolted upright and looked around. In the dim light he could see that Mouse and Betsy were awake and sitting up. He gazed at Evie. She looked like she was still asleep. She must be still trapped in the dream, in that creepy clearing, with the shadows closing in on her. Except that now she would be all alone.

'Evie!' He grabbed her and shook her hard. After a second or two she woke suddenly, breathing heavily, her eyes wide.

'What on earth are you doing now?' Jack's mum yelled. 'Why are you waking up Evie, for goodness sake? This is just ridiculous. I've never heard such a racket – in the middle of night! This is the last time you're having friends round, Jack O'Reilly. Now go to back to sleep, all of you.'

Jack had learnt how to block out his mother so that her grating voice was reduced to a hum in the background. He waited until she had left the room before he spoke. 'Evie,' he whispered. 'Evie, you were the last one left in the dream. Are you all right? What happened? Did you see anything?'

Her eyes were fearful. 'It was so dark, but I could hear the creatures and see their teeth flashing. And then, just as I woke up, I heard a strange noise. Something was hissing at me. And I felt the flap of a huge wing against my face.'

CHAPTER SEVENTEEN

It wasn't until Monday that the Dream Squad was able to discuss the events of Friday night.

Jack's mum had been cross but Jack had managed to persuade her not to say anything to the others' parents. She'd agreed reluctantly, but insisted there would be no more sleepovers for a long time. What she really meant was that she didn't think the four of them should hang out together any more as she suspected something strange was going on, but she didn't say this out loud.

When the bell rang for morning break, Jack legged it to the reading tree, desperate to speak to the others. It was all he had thought about for the entire weekend. On the plus side, they had achieved something incredible by meeting up in a dream. That was mind-blowing. But on the other hand, the dream had somehow turned into a nightmare. He needed to know how and why this had happened.

Jack's dreams were positive most of the time. Sometimes they had challenging elements, or they were frustrating because he couldn't quite get to where he wanted, but he had never experienced a nightmare like the one they'd had on Friday night. He was starting to feel nervous about what they had started, and wondering whether this whole dream business was bigger than he had imagined.

The others were waiting for him at the reading tree. Betsy had been doing her research again and was carrying some folded sheets of paper and a couple of books. 'I've been reading more about lucid dreaming, trying to understand what happened to us,' she explained. 'Apparently, with lucid dreams, you must not only be aware that you're dreaming. You must also have a clear memory of the waking world the whole time. Did you all find that was true? Could you remember the real world?'

'Yes,' nodded Mouse.

'Me too,' said Jack. 'Except usually I feel that I can control what's happening. I can sort of *will* things to happen by imagining them or focusing really hard on something. But this time – well it was different. It was like I had no control. Those shadows, the noises… it was like they weren't in my head, but they were coming from somewhere else.'

'Exactly,' agreed Mouse. 'That's what I felt too. I was trying to think of other things. I wanted to stop it, but I couldn't.'

Evie, who had been very quiet up until now, said softly: 'I think we're getting into something that could be dangerous. Something we don't fully understand.'

Betsy seemed not to hear her and went on shuffling through her papers. 'Listen to this,' she said. 'Researchers have examined dream control and dream awareness and found out that while they often go together, one can occur without the other…'

'What on earth does THAT mean?' asked Mouse.

Jack frowned. 'I think it means that even if you are aware you are dreaming, you can't necessarily control what happens.'

'That's right!' exclaimed Betsy.

'Does it say anything about what are you meant to do if you find yourself in a nightmare?' asked Jack.

'Well, it says here that you need to use your lucid *powers* to destroy it. You can walk out of it or wake yourself up, but the most effective thing to do is to find out what it represents and why it scares you. Then you can conquer the nightmare by facing your fears.' Betsy paused and looked around at the others. 'So you see what this means? If we are afraid, we can get stuck in a nightmare. But if we understand why we are afraid and remind ourselves that it is just a dream, we can face our fears and overcome them.'

'But...' pondered Mouse, 'that wasn't my nightmare. It was all new to me. It must have been someone else's thoughts. Someone else's nightmare.'

'Yes, it was mine,' said Evie quietly.

Everyone looked at her. She blushed a deep scarlet and looked at the floor. 'It's just that...well...I've had that nightmare since I was a child. I usually have it once every few months, the same dream, being in a clearing full of shadows, with creatures circling and coming closer, and the growling...I wasn't thinking about it, but it must have been there, somewhere in my subconscious, and I couldn't stop it. Once we were in that forest and the thought crossed my mind, that was it. I realised what was happening and I tried very hard to stop it, but I couldn't. It just seemed to spiral out of control.'

She stopped. There was silence, apart from the noise of children running around the playground and shouting, which seemed so distant it could have been happening on another planet.

'I'm sorry,' Evie whispered, under her breath.

Again there was silence. Eventually Jack spoke up. 'Well it wasn't your fault. It wasn't as though you meant it to happen.'

'It could have happened to anyone,' agreed Betsy. 'All of us have fears and nightmares, right?'

Evie looked inconsolable and stared at the ground.

'Wait!' said Mouse. 'This means that we can cure you of your nightmare. Remember - all you have to do is to be aware that you are dreaming and not be afraid. You need to gain mastery over your fears. If you're not afraid, and you know it's just a nightmare, it can't touch you. You'll never need to be scared of it again.'

CHAPTER EIGHTEEN

Despite what had happened, the gang did not want to give up on their dreaming adventures. They were not prepared to throw it all away because of one bad experience. It was Jack who convinced them. 'We can't stop now,' he insisted. 'We just have to work out how to control the dreams better.'

'Okay,' said Evie cautiously. 'But if we're going to keep going, then we need to understand what went wrong and make sure that it doesn't happen again. I mean, what if...what if we were to get stuck in a nightmare and never wake up? Or if one of us was to get hurt in a nightmare?'

Mouse shuddered at the thought, but Betsy, practical as ever, jumped in: 'That is scientifically impossible. A dream is still a dream, even if we are aware of what is happening. We couldn't actually injure ourselves. Whatever is happening in the dream, it can't stop us waking up...' She trailed off, sounding less sure of herself than she usually did.

'Look,' said Jack. 'A few weeks ago, we had no idea that any of this was possible. True, we could be opening up a can of worms here, but we mustn't be scared. We have to explore it fearlessly and remain open to the possibilities. That's what Great Granny Georgia has always told me.'

So they made a plan. They arranged to meet in each other's dreams two nights a week. Before they left school on the chosen days, they picked a place they could focus on in their dream, somewhere to find each other.

They also agreed on an object to look for, something to unite them in their dream world, their "anchor" object. The idea was that it would draw them into the same dream. Then each of them would drink some of the special dream herbs before bed and sink into sleep.

More often than not it worked, and they all met up in each other's dreams as planned. They took it in turns to choose the place and the anchor object, so that each had a chance to lead the others into their own private dream world.

CHAPTER NINETEEN

Mouse loved fairy tales, so he took the others on a grand tour of fairy tale dreams. They climbed Jack's beanstalk, mined gold with the seven dwarves and rescued princesses from towers. They discovered gingerbread houses in the forest, went to glamorous balls, rode in carriages and escaped from wizards and witches. Although many of the stories had a dark side, the Dream Squad was not afraid. The dreams never turned into nightmares. This was because the stories were so familiar to them. They knew what to expect and, and they knew their adventures would have a happy ending. They felt in control and didn't need to worry about how things would turn out.

Mouse didn't tell the others, but the reason he loved dreaming about fairy tales was that his mother used to read them to him. Dreaming about them made him feel close to her. They made him feel safe and happy. He remembered curling up in bed with his head on his mother's lap, breathing in her flowery scent, listening to her soft voice as she read from a big picture book.

Mostly Mouse just dreamt about the fairytales themselves, often playing one of the main characters, but on one occasion he saw his mother. She had the picture book on her lap, just as she used to, and she was stroking his hair. She had smiled at him, such a warm, loving smile that Mouse felt it engulf him in a soft glow. He didn't know if the others were there at the time, but he didn't think they were, because all he had felt was the strong, all-encompassing presence of his mother.

Evie loved nature, especially anything water-related. She showed the Dream Squad beautiful beaches and oceans. Sometimes she took them to rivers and mountains *and forests. They picked wild flowers and ate delicious picnic spreads with animals all around them.*

Evie often dreamt that she was an animal herself. She loved these dreams because she felt so free. She was not confined by the limitations of her human body, which she always found to be quite cumbersome and clumsy in real life. She had dreams where she roamed as a wolf in the mountains. In others she was a bear pounding through the woods. Once she dreamt she was a tiny beetle on a flower, crawling over the giant petals and sliding down the stalk. Her favourite dreams were when she was a sea creature – a fish, a whale or a shark. Once she had spent the night as a dolphin, leaping and diving in the surf.

Betsy was fascinated by history and science, and her dreams usually involved travel of some sort – often time travel. She particularly loved dreaming about medieval times, with knights and castles, jousting tournaments, warlords and crusades. Once she watched from the water's edge as King Arthur was given Excalibur by the Lady of the Lake. Her bedroom was stacked with books and pictures from those times. The olden days filled her dreams as well as her books.

And Jack's dreams – they always came back to climbing and flying; conquering mountains and then soaring free over the land below. The others hadn't tried flying in their dreams before, so this was something new and exciting for them. It was a sensation they all enjoyed - though none quite as much as Jack.

While they practiced dreaming with each other, they also worked on finding techniques that would help them to stay in or leave a dream. Jack felt this was important. He wanted to find out how to be certain of waking from a dream if things took a sinister turn. If they could figure this out, they need never be frightened of nightmares. At the same time, there might be things they could do to help them stay longer in a dream they were enjoying.

Jack had noticed that there were often signs that he was about to wake up. The dream started to feel "unstable" and he would begin to notice sensations from the real world – usually noises. Then he knew the dream was coming to an end. But he had also discovered that if he rubbed his hands together, or focused on carrying on with whatever he was doing, he could prolong the dream.

The children's hopes and dreams were all different, but sharing them allowed them to explore each other's secret worlds and to discover their greatest longings. They became closer and felt that there was an unspoken bond between them. Dreams, they realised, were a place where all their innermost desires and untold secrets came to the surface - along with, as the Dream Squad was soon to discover, their deepest, darkest fears.

CHAPTER TWENTY

As their dream worlds became more adventurous, things in the "real" world became increasingly challenging. Miss Longbottom had cottoned onto their secret meetings and was hot on their trail. She seemed to have made it her mission to destroy their little group. It became harder and harder to evade her.

At first she separated them whenever she could, putting one or two of them in detention and ensuring they were always in different rooms. The first time she discovered them under the reading tree she had crept up and swept aside the weeping willow branches triumphantly as though expecting to catch them with stolen booty. She seemed quite disappointed when she realised they were just sitting in a circle, talking. But her eyes blazed when she saw the book on Betsy's lap and she whipped it away in a fury. Then she gave them all a week's detention and banned them from sitting under the reading tree again.

As if that wasn't bad enough, the children found to their horror the next morning that all the beautiful branches of the reading tree had been sawn off, leaving only the bare naked trunk and a few little stumps. They agreed that it was too risky to keep meeting at school now that Miss Longbottom was becoming suspicious. This made it much more difficult for them to coordinate and discuss their dreams. They met up after school whenever they could, trying to snatch a few minutes here and there, but their parents were still wary after the sleepover incident.

They started leaving each other secret notes outlining their dream plans. Jack called these their "Dream Maps". There was a danger these could be intercepted, of course, but there didn't seem to be any other option. Besides, it was unlikely that anyone else would be able to work out what they meant. So Jack would hand the other three their Dream Maps on the two days of the week they planned to dream together. These maps outlined where and when they would meet that night and any other details they needed to know.

One day Jack slipped everyone their Dream Map as usual:

Meeting Place: St Bartholomew's School (at the end of the street)
Anchor Object: a boat
Time: 9 pm tonight

That particular day, however, Mouse's Dream Map disappeared. One minute it was tucked safely away in his pocket; or at least he could have sworn it was. The next minute, it was gone. Mouse searched for it frantically, re-tracing his steps from his locker, to the classroom, to the playground, and then back again, but he couldn't find it anywhere. He felt uneasy, but tried to assure himself that it didn't matter. After all, he could remember the instructions and he told himself that the piece of paper must have just fallen out somewhere. The school cleaner would probably pick it up and throw it in a bin. No one would know what it meant anyway.

Still, he felt uncomfortable and he decided not to mention it to the others.

That was when things really started to hot up in the dream world.

CHAPTER TWENTY-ONE

That night, the Dream Squad met up at the allocated place.
They were getting better at finding each other and aligning their dreams. It was happening more quickly each time they tried it.

There was usually a slight discrepancy in the timings, of course, because of the impossibility of them all falling asleep at a set time - all the more so when they were trying hard to do exactly that. It was rather like Christmas Eve. On that night children are desperate to fall asleep so that the coast is clear for Father Christmas, but most lie awake far longer than usual, almost bursting with anticipation. That's rather what it was like for the Dream Squad each time they arranged to meet up in a dream.

Jack was the most efficient at falling asleep. He'd had the most practice at dreaming and knew exactly how long it would take him to doze off. He instantly recognized the feelings of drifting into another world. He would go to bed at 8 pm, switch off his light at 8.30 pm and be confident of falling asleep by 9 pm. That was unless music was blaring out from his sister's room and his mum was yelling at her to turn it down. That usually delayed things.

Mouse found it more difficult. Sometimes he was still awake after 9.30 pm, tossing and turning in his bed, worrying about the adventures he was missing. Betsy was pretty regimental about her bedtime routine and was good at reaching the dream world on time. Evie always took longer than she meant. She'd be settled in bed and suddenly remember she'd forgotten to brush her teeth, or close the curtains, or get her clothes ready for the next day. She often got up several times before finally settling down, so that despite her good intentions she was frequently the last one to arrive in the dream.

Anyway, on this particular night, they all went to bed buzzing with anticipation and ready to head to the school and focus on their anchor object - a boat.

CHAPTER TWENTY-TWO

Evie was the last to arrive as usual. She found the others standing together looking up the street near their school. Except that the street wasn't paved as it was in real life. The pavement was a river and there were boats tethered to the lampposts.

'Ha, well, at least we know we're definitely dreaming,' said Mouse.

'Ooh, I've always wanted to go to school on a boat!' exclaimed Evie.

Jack jumped into the first boat and Evie followed him into it. Betsy and Mouse climbed into the boat behind them. Seconds later they were whooshing down the river, being carried on the fast-flowing current, until they arrived at the front door of the school.

'It's so strange,' said Mouse. 'Everything looks so…. so real, but it's completely different at the same time.'

They climbed out of the boats and pushed open the school door. They peered into the office. It was empty and silent. So were the corridors and classrooms.

'Let's go and see if our lockers are in the same place,' said Betsy.

They ran past their classroom and each found their locker, exactly where it should be. Mouse opened his locker and found it over-flowing with sweets. He chuckled sheepishly. 'I didn't even realize I was imagining that!'

'Let's go and check the assembly hall,' said Jack, leading the way down the corridor. On their way, they passed Miss Longbottom's office. Jack hesitated. Something made him want to open the door. Until that point the dream had been fun. Now the atmosphere had turned sinister.

'It's a bit eerie, isn't it?' whispered Evie.

As she said this, they heard a rasping noise and the flapping of wings from inside Miss Longbottom's office. Mouse shuddered and let out a yelp that sounded like the cry of a terrified, wounded animal. The others looked round and saw to their amazement that he was completely naked.

Poor Mouse – his face turned bright scarlet and his mouth gaped open like a fish out of water. He seemed to be struggling to breathe as he searched for something to cover himself.

Betsy and Evie looked away, feeling embarrassed. Jack knew he had to say something. 'Mouse, don't forget this is just a dream. This is one of your fears, but if you face it, it can't hurt you.'

Mouse nodded, but he couldn't find any words. He scurried into a corner and tried to hide himself from the others by pressing against the wall.

'Wait, what's that noise? Can you hear that?' asked Evie.

'What IS that…?' Jack's voice echoed around the corridors in a way that made them all feel anxious.

'Shhhhhh', said Betsy, straining to hear. It seemed to be coming from the chemistry lab, and it sounded as if someone was calling for help. The cries became louder as they crept down the corridor towards the lab, scared of what they might find. Mouse, still naked, followed them, pinning himself to the wall.

Jack opened the lab door and the children looked in cautiously. To their shock they saw their chemistry teacher, Mr Burley, standing with his back to them by the blackboard. This was the first time they had encountered another person since they'd started dreaming together.

'Mr Burley?' Jack whispered.

Mr Burley turned slowly towards them, and as he did so the children gasped in horror. His arms were tied to the desk with thick metal chains. Beyond him they *glimpsed a large black creature in the shadows. The creature gave a threatening hiss. It seemed to be guarding him.*

Mr Burley looked at the children and opened his mouth, but no sound came out. Jack took an involuntary step backwards. The creature (was it a giant bird?) hissed again. Jack realised that Mr Burley was silently mouthing the word 'Help'. Then the old teacher turned his head slightly and stared at the blackboard. The children watched as numbers began to appear on the board in white chalk as though being scrawled there by an invisible hand: 5 – 9 – 2 – 3 – 9 – 4.

Jack stared at the numbers, whispering them under his breath. 5 – 9 – 2 – 3 – 9 – 4. He repeated the sequence, trying to commit it to his memory. He didn't know what the numbers meant, but he was sure they were important.

At that moment, however, Betsy disappeared. She usually woke up first. Her mum made her set her alarm for 7 am so that she could help with her baby brother before school. The others realised they didn't have much time left. Time was always different in the dream world. It became warped and didn't seem to follow normal rules. Some dreams felt as though they went on for days. Others were over in what seemed like a flash.

Jack felt a clenching in the pit of his stomach. What was Mr Burley doing there? And how were they meant to help him? He turned to the others. 'Quick, we're running out of time. We're going to wake up soon. What do we do?'

There was no answer. He spun around and saw that he was the only child left. Only Mr Burley was still there, looking at him with pleading eyes. Jack felt helpless. He rubbed his hands together frantically, but everything around him was starting to shake. The dream was slipping away. 5 – 9 – 2 - 3 – 9 – 4. He heard another hiss and the flap of wings, and then he sat up in bed. Breathing heavily, he scribbled the six numbers down on the back page of his dream journal. Then he lay back and tried to make sense of what had happened.

Chapter Twenty-Three

Mr Burley was as ancient as they come, or at least he seemed that way to the children. He had wiry grey hair that poked out of his head at strange angles, and his arms and legs dangled awkwardly from his body as though they had been sewn on. He was like an old scarecrow that has been patched together. His thin face and bony cheeks made him look malnourished. Betsy had heard her mum say he could do with fattening up. She'd joked that Mr Burly was positively scrawny, not *burly* at all. Yet he had a kind face, with gentle eyes beneath his thick-rimmed glasses. All the children cherished Mr Burley, as he was the only teacher who always had time for them. That was even true of the unruly kids and the ones that answered back and played tricks on him and didn't do their homework. He seemed to have unlimited reserves of patience and compassion.

Mr Burley loved doing experiments in his classes, but the older he got, the more dangerous they became. He kept shifting his glasses higher up his nose as he tried to see what he was doing. Last week he had blown up a Bunsen burner. He had scorched his eyebrows and burnt some whiskers off his face, but it didn't seem to faze him.

Afterwards Jack had overheard Miss Longbottom speaking to her assistant Mrs Daisy in the corridor: 'The man's completely mad – the ghastly old fool needs to come with a hazard warning!' She spoke with such venom that flecks of spittle shot out from the corners of her mouth.

Jack suspected the real reason she hated him was because she was always so kind to the children. She always looked on the verge of retching whenever she caught him being nice to them. Sometimes he even tried to protect the children from Miss Longbottom's verbal onslaughts and would ask her not to punish them. This would cause Miss Longbottom to turn an unhealthy shade of purple as she tried to suppress her fury.

It seemed the strangest thing in the world that Mr Burley had appeared in their dream. How had he got there? And why was he tied up and calling for help? What did the number on the blackboard mean? And wait - why on earth had Mouse suddenly lost his clothes?

Strange things were starting to happen in their dream realm and Jack sensed they were losing control.

Chapter Twenty-Four

The next day the children ventured nervously into school, wandering what would happen when they saw Mr Burley in person. Would he acknowledge them? Had he actually seen them in the dream? Was it his dream too or was it just theirs?

They had to get through the whole morning first, because chemistry wasn't until the afternoon. Time dragged by slowly. They managed to have a quick conversation at lunchtime, and Jack noticed that Mouse was quieter and more fidgety than usual.

'Mouse, last night... why... why do you think that happened?' Jack asked.

Mouse reddened. 'I don't know,' he murmured. 'Well, I mean...I used to have this dream when I was younger. It was when I started school... soon after my mum died. I had this recurring dream...I would be in class, and everything seemed normal, and then suddenly I'd look down and realise I was naked. It was awful. Everyone was laughing at me.' Mouse looked at the ground and for a moment his eyes filled with tears.

Betsy patted his arm tenderly, if a little awkwardly.

Mouse managed a half-smile. 'I haven't had the dream for years though. I thought it had gone for good.' He shuddered. 'Last night it was so much more vivid...so real.'

'It's strange your nightmare came back,' said Betsy. 'I wonder why. Maybe it was something to do with being at school in the dream.'

'It was as though the dream took a sinister turn and then everything changed,' said Jack. 'It happened just as we walked past Miss Longbottom's office. That's when you lost your clothes. And that's when we heard Mr Burley calling for help...'

'Yes, Mr Burley,' said Betsy. 'That was so weird... and the number on the blackboard, what on earth did that mean? Do you think we should we say anything to him?'

'We all saw him, didn't we?' replied Jack. 'And he saw us too. It's not as though we imagined it.'

'Well, we could have conjured him up ourselves, couldn't we?' said Evie. 'Just because he was in our dream doesn't mean that it was his dream as well.' She paused, feeling confused. 'We can't exactly go up and ask him, can we? He'll think we're mad.'

Jack scratched his head. 'Maybe we should give him ... some sort of sign? If he's on the same page, then he'll respond to us'

'What sort of sign?' asked Evie.

Before they could discuss the matter any further, the bell rang and they piled into the chemistry lab. Jack could hardly wait to set eyes on Mr Burley - except that Mr Burley wasn't there. Instead Miss Longbottom was sitting at the front of the lab, her wide bottom spilling over the edges of her chair.

'Children', she snarled. 'Mr Burley' – globules of saliva landed on the desk in front of her as she spat out the name – 'Mr Burley is unwell today. I will be in charge while you do your work. I require you to copy out chapters one to fifteen of your textbooks, including the diagrams, before the bell rings. If not, you can finish in detention.'

There was a gasp of horror. Fifteen chapters? That was almost seventy pages! The bell would be ringing in forty minutes – it was impossible.

Miss Longbottom's lips curled into a horrible smile. 'Now get on with it,' she cried.

Half an hour later, as the class scribbled in their notebooks in silence, there was a tentative tap on the door. Miss Longbottom's head snapped up crossly. She marched over to the door and opened it. Mrs Daisy was standing there. The children heard Miss Longbottom hiss: 'What do you want?' Then she went out into the corridor and shut the door behind her.

Jack could hear the low murmur of their voices but it was impossible to make out what they were saying. He crept up to the lab door and put his ear to it. Yes, he could hear them now. Mrs Daisy was saying: 'His family... they say that he just won't wake up, you see, but they don't know what has happened... so strange... poor - '.

Something must have made Miss Longbottom suspicious because at that moment she suddenly opened the door again. She glared at Jack. 'What are you doing, boy?'

'I need the loo, Miss Longbottom,' Jack said hurriedly.

'You'll go when I say you can go,' snarled Miss Longbottom. 'Now go back to your desk or you'll be on double detention for the rest of the week'.

Jack wasn't sure what double detention was, but he didn't like the sound of it. He went back to his desk and sat down, glancing at Evie and Betsy, who were sitting in front of him. Evie raised her eyebrows questioningly, but they both knew they'd have to wait before they could talk properly. Jack looked down at his textbook, his mind racing. All he could think about was Mr Burley. What had happened to him and was his absence linked to their dream the night before? And how were they supposed to help him?

CHAPTER TWENTY-FIVE

As the Dream Squad's unspoken leader, the one who had started it all, Jack felt responsible for the others. It was not until the bell rang for the end of the school, and the entire class began to trudge to the detention room, that he had a thought. He was surprised it had not occurred to him before. 'We need to talk to my Great Granny Georgia,' he whispered to the others. 'We need to tell her everything. She knows so much about this stuff. She'll know exactly what to do.'

The Dream Squad made arrangements to see her that weekend. They told their parents they were going to Jack's house for the day and Jack told his mum he was going to see Great Granny Georgia. His mum was too busy arguing with Bella to take much notice. 'Make sure you're back for dinner,' was all she said. Jack nodded and hurried to the station where he met the rest of the squad.

Great Granny Georgia lived an hour away on the train. During the journey Jack told the others about the weekends he had spent magic dreaming at her house. They listened avidly and felt relieved that they would be able to talk to an adult about this whole business - an adult who would believe them.

Great Granny Georgia ushered them into her cluttered living room. They settled themselves on cushions on the floor because all the chairs were piled high with random objects – books, ornaments, and little trinkets. Great Granny Georgia had a neat grey bun and a lined face.

When she smiled, her eyes sank into her face and almost disappeared in a sea of wrinkles. She bustled around in the kitchen for a few minutes. They heard cups clinking and a kettle whistling. She emerged carrying a tray with four cups of warm milk, a cup of tea for herself, and a plate of raisin oatmeal cookies. She passed round the drinks before moving a pile of junk from an old grey armchair in the corner of the room. A cloud of dust rose from the chair as she sat down and made herself comfortable.

Then she listened to their story. Jack took the lead, and the others chipped in with the parts they thought were important. They told her about the first 'dream' meeting between Jack and Evie; how the others had taught themselves to dream lucidly; how they began to dream together, and how the dream on the glacier had turned into Evie's nightmare. They described their dream maps and anchor objects and dream journals. They told her how their latest dream had taken a sinister twist; how Mouse had lost his clothes and how they had seen Mr Burley tied up in the classroom calling for help and the six-digit number that had appeared on the blackboard. They told her about Mr Burley being absent from school the next day.

Great Granny Georgia didn't interrupt. She just listened intently.

CHAPTER TWENTY-SIX

fter the children had finished talking, Great Granny Georgia was silent for a long time. She was so quiet that Jack became worried. He began to wonder about the wisdom of having told her everything. Would she think they had taken things too far by meeting up in their dreams? Would she think they had been courting trouble? And, above all, would she be able to help?

At last Great Granny Georgia took a deep breath, a mixture of a murmur and a sigh. 'This is all quite fascinating. You have discovered the world of conscious, controlled dreaming. Not only that, you have taken it a step further and crossed into multiple dream worlds, entering each other's consciousness. That's very impressive, you know. Many people spend their whole lives trying to learn about the dream world. They try desperately to remember and interpret their dreams, to understand what they mean and to learn from them. But usually they never truly understand the dream world and very rarely do they gain mastery over it.

'I am not entirely surprised that you have achieved so much, though. It is well known that children can tap into their dream worlds much more easily than adults. Their brains are still developing. They are primed to explore other worlds and other realms of consciousness.

'I'll tell you the main thing that prevents children from exploring their dream worlds to the full. It's adults. Adults don't understand about dreaming, and so they shrug off children's night-time adventures. They give them explanations. They soothe away the nightmares and brush off the vivid dreams. They don't encourage children to explore and understand this other world.

'Very few adults realise that our dream worlds are as real and important as our waking worlds. But when you think about it, why should one be more real than the other? That's why I've been encouraging you to dream since you were little, Jack. I didn't want your dream explorations to be stifled in any way. I wanted you to keep your mind open so that you could experience the true wonders of this other world. The only thing is, I didn't expect you to bring your friends along on the ride too! How wonderful...I've only read a couple of other accounts of people who've managed to experience each other's dream worlds. Of course, there are bound to be more who have achieved it, but scientists dismiss their claims as nonsense. After all, how can they prove it? That's the thing these days. It's all about science and evidence and proof. So things like a dream universe get written off as twaddle.'

Jack interrupted: 'So you do believe us?'

'Of course I do! I can tell that you are all being honest about your experiences. I've no doubt that many other children have done the same as you, but they don't mention it to adults because they don't think that they'd be believed.'

'Why are adults so disbelieving?' asked Mouse.

'Well... think of it like this. When you are a child, there are so many options, so many things to believe in. But there comes a point when people's brains start to shift into adult mode. They become increasingly set in their ways and close themselves off to possibilities. The change usually happens gradually, so that people don't notice it taking place.

Then, one day, they find themselves leading a boring, predictable life. They've become disbelieving, cynical even, and have left behind all their hopes and dreams for excitement and exploration. We think our brains grow as we get older, but in many ways they do the opposite - they shrink. They become closed off to opportunities and ideas. You have to fight against it if you are to stop it happening. You have to fight to keep dreaming.'

The children mulled over what she had said. Jack asked: 'What about the nightmare we had? What do you think happened? Evie's nightmare and Mouse's nightmare coming back as well… we can't figure it out. Why are these nightmares appearing out of nowhere when we love dreaming together?'

Great Granny stroked the wiry grey hairs on the end of her chin. 'Hmm… well I do remember reading about this once. Most people who discover the dream world only use it positively. They want to broaden their minds and explore different realms. They want to understand their alternative realities. But every so often someone comes along with less pure intentions. Dreams, you see, are very powerful things. They reflect a person's deepest beliefs and hope. But as with everything powerful, there is a dark side. Dreams also capture people's doubts and worries. And there is no better way to gain power and control over others than to be able to tap into their deepest fears. There are even dream herbs that help people tap into the dark side of the dream world. They encourage shadowy terrors to enter your dream consciousness and take over.'

Jack shuddered. Great Granny Georgia placed a reassuring hand on his arm and said: 'It's all right, Jack. There aren't many people who use dreams in a bad way…though I do wonder if perhaps you have come across someone who does…'

Great Granny Georgia stared into the distance for a moment. 'Actually, I've just remembered. I have a very interesting book about this exact topic – the dark side of the dream world. I'll fetch it from the bookshelf.'

'Wait,' said Jack. 'So, you're saying that someone could be deliberately trying to get into our dreams and turn them into nightmares? To gain some sort of control over us? Who on earth would want to do that?'

The children looked at each other as the answer hit them all at the same time.

CHAPTER TWENTY-SEVEN

'**M**iss Longbottom!'

They all spoke her name at once.

Great Granny Georgia gazed from one to another. 'So you think you know who's trying to infiltrate your dreams and turn them into nightmares?'

'Yes,' said Jack firmly. 'It has to be our headmistress, Miss Longbottom.'

'She's a terror,' said Evie.

'A real witch', added Betsy.

'She hates all the children in the school, and most of the teachers too,' said Jack. 'I heard her say the other day how much she hated Mr Burley and wanted to get rid of him – now he's disappeared and we saw him tied up in our dream. She has to be behind all of this!'

'She's always punishing children and loves watching them squirm', said Mouse. 'And she keeps a bird in her office that no one has ever seen. It makes a raspy, hissing sound.'

Great Granny looked at Mouse sharply. 'You say she has a bird?'

'Yes, she keeps it hidden in a cage in her office. We can hear it sometimes and we've seen its big black feathers.'

'Do you think the bird has something to do with all this?' asked Jack.

Great Granny Georgia stroked her whiskers again. 'Birds are very significant in dreams. Generally, they are positive symbols. They can point to your goals, aspirations and hopes. They also reflect harmony, balance and love.'

She scrutinised the children's faces. 'However, not all birds carry happiness and joy. A bird with black feathers can signify death. It only appears in a dream when something is dead or decaying and about to die. The most dangerous birds in the dream world are Black Vultures. They are vicious and evil. They make raspy, hissing sounds when they are feeding or fighting. Seeing a black vulture in your dream is a very bad sign. I've heard it said that a black vulture is the only bird that can fly with ease across the boundary between the awake world to the dream world – carrying nightmares on its wings.'

'So wait – you're saying that it can cross from the awake world to the dream world?' Evie asked.

'Apparently so. If this terrible woman keeps a black vulture…well, it can't be a coincidence. She must be using this bird to spread fear in the dream world and to open the door to people's nightmares.'

'Poor Mr Burley,' added Evie. 'Miss Longbottom hated him because he was always so kind to us. She can't stand anyone being kind to children'.

'But what has she done with him?' Mouse asked.

'Hmm…' Great Granny Georgia tugged one of her whiskers so hard that Jack thought she might pull it out. 'From what you've told me, this could be a case of "dream trapping". If so, you have come across an extremely rare phenomenon. It requires great power and truly evil intent. I have heard of it happening only once before. It's a story that is passed down through the generations to remind children to respect the power of the dream world. I've always thought it might have been a made-up story…but now I'm not so sure.'

'Tell us the story,' said Mouse.

'Well, I don't want to scare you, but I suppose it's important for you to know what you're dealing with…'

CHAPTER TWENTY-EIGHT

The Story of Eliza Wood

Eliza Wood was said to be one of the most skilled magic dreamers to have ever lived. People claimed she had been able to dream since she was born, but when you think about it, how could they have known that? Still, by the time she was five, she had apparently visited many of the dream realms and had learnt to explore deeper into the dream world than many did in their entire life.

By the time she was seven, Eliza had taught her close friends how to meet her in their dreams and they would explore different realms together. Every night was a new adventure and Eliza began to keep a beautiful book where she recounted all her escapades while asleep.

When she turned ten, Eliza started to meet other famous dreamers in their dream worlds. Around that time, there were a few big names in the field, you see, people who were revered as experts of the discipline. Most were associated with a particular specialty.

There was Professor Gerhard in Austria - he was known to be one of the most skilled leaders in focused dreaming. It was said that he could focus on a place he wanted to visit in his dream and he would arrive at that exact location within seconds of falling asleep. Of course, this was somewhat difficult to prove unless another dreamer was waiting there for him.

There was also a scientist from Poland, Magda Malinski, who was the world master of interpreting Dream Signs and Symbols, particularly in cases of recurring *dreams. She often used these to predict occurrences in people's lives and on occasion she foretold major world events with remarkable accuracy.*

Then there was Dr Maria Dolores, a Spanish dreamer who became an expert in the process of object transference between the real world and the dream world. In other words, she worked out how her actions in the dream world could impact on the real world. Scientific researchers tested this by setting her tasks while she was asleep – apparently she was very successful. For example, they would tell her to move objects to specific places in the dream world and they would then watch them appear in that very same place in the real world. Now remember, the dream world and the waking world are separate dimensions so this was an impressive feat – it seemed that Maria Dolores had located the exact point at which the two dimensions intersected.

One time, it was said, Dr Dolores went to Buckingham Palace in her dream and left a cup of tea on the King's bedside table so that it was waiting for him when she woke up. This was never verified by the King or any of the palace officials, but many people believed that the cup of tea really had materialized.

Maria Dolores also wrote extensively on the use of anchor objects in lucid dreaming – she always focused on a particular object to assist her in reaching her destination and she discovered lots of little tricks for making this process easier and more effective. Apparently, the night she visited the Queen, Maria Dolores had drawn a cup of tea and an outline of the Palace on her arm before she went to sleep and this helped to guide her there once she was dreaming.

Of course, Maria Dolores and the other famous dreamers back at that time all had good intent. They were simply fascinated by the process of dreaming and wanted to see how far they could push the boundaries between the real world and the dream world. They had no desire to cause harm.

In hindsight, perhaps it was only a matter of time – as it seems to be with all human discovery – that these powers fell into the hands of someone who wanted to use them for evil.

So back to Eliza Wood.... each night while she slept, Eliza met up with all of these famous dreamers and many more. She learnt their skills and absorbed their knowledge with astonishing efficiency. At the rate she was going she was set to become the most powerful dreamer in the world before she even reached her teenage years.

It was around the time of her twelfth birthday, so the story goes, that she became friends with an evil dreamer. An old man who went by the name of Spiky Jake.

Spiky Jake was something of a loner and had been obsessed with the dream world all his life. He spent his days in his basement, trying to recreate night-time and learning how to magic dream. For a long time he wasn't very successful and didn't seem to have the ability to tap into that part of his mind. Some people just don't have the right type of brain, apparently.

The endless hours spent in his basement, away from other people and natural light, began to have an effect on Spiky Jake. He started to go funny in the head. He refused to accept that he couldn't become powerful in the dream realm and, as it happened, he started to make some progress. It took him years, though. Years of being alone - and then he only managed to develop the skills to harness the dark powers of the night.

When Spiky Jake heard about Eliza Wood he became insanely jealous. He thought it unfair that such a young girl had been able to master the dream world so effortlessly, whereas he had had to spend all those years in a dark basement getting nowhere. Intent on learning her secrets, he befriended her and her family. Discovering that she had a love of music, he introduced himself as Jacob and offered to give her piano lessons. Eliza and her parents were thrilled. No one suspected he had ill intentions.

Once Spiky Jake had gained Eliza's trust he got her to tell him about her dream skills. He learnt about her secrets and her fears too. Then one day, he managed to sneak into Eliza's bedroom after a piano lesson and steal her dream book from under her pillow. This gave him real power over her and from there the situation quickly went downhill. It wasn't long before Spiky Jake had conquered Eliza's dream world. She started to have nightmares. Terrible nightmares, night after night. She went from being happy and bubbly to being withdrawn, nervous and exhausted.

Then one day, she simply didn't wake up.

She hadn't died, mind you; she just stayed asleep.

Spiky Jake had been so jealous of her dream talents that he managed to trap her in a nightmare from which she couldn't wake up.

On the same day, Spiky Jake disappeared and was never seen again.

Eliza's parents were distraught, of course. Doctors and specialists came from all around the world, but no one could find anything wrong with little Eliza Wood. She wasn't unwell or in a coma. She was simply sleeping. Her brain still seemed to be active. She just wouldn't wake up.

Reporters from across the globe queued at her front door, shouting out questions to her parents and trying to get a glimpse of Eliza herself. She was already well known in the dreamers' world, but now she became famous across the rest of the world too. Everyone knew of Eliza Wood — the little girl who couldn't wake up.

Eventually the ruckus died down. Eliza's parents moved to a cottage by the sea. They put Eliza in a comfy bed, with a window overlooking the ocean. Years passed, and Eliza grew into a little old woman, still sleeping in the same bed.

It is said that she spent the rest of her life sleeping, trapped in the nightmare that Spiky Jake had made for her.

CHAPTER TWENTY-NINE

Great Granny Georgia finished the story and tried to smile reassuringly. 'As I said, I don't want to frighten you. It's probably just a load of bunkum…some story that was made up by someone's sister's brother's great-aunt and got passed down from generation to generation. Besides, even if it's true, it's perfectly possible that Eliza had a very happy life in her dream world.' Great Granny Georgia did not sound too convinced about this.

'Anyway,' she hurried on, 'it's the only story of its kind I've ever heard. For someone to have so much power in the dream world that they could actually stop a person from waking up, well, it would be extremely rare…'

She stood up and started rummaging around a dusty bookshelf beside the window. It took her a while to find what she was looking for…a small book with faded red lettering on its black cover. She handed it to Jack. 'Take this and study it. And then come up with a plan.'

Jack traced his finger over the red lettering on the cover.

'*Control Your Nightmares*', Betsy read out loud over his shoulder.

'But I don't understand,' said Evie. 'If it IS Miss Longbottom, how is she getting access to our dreams in the first place?'

'Well…' said Great Granny Georgia, rubbing her chin again. 'She must have picked up some information about you somehow. Information is power. Remember when Spikey Jake got hold of Eliza's dream book?

Once Miss Longbottom knows where you are going and what you are doing in your dreams, she can start to exert her power and control. Is there any way that she could have found out what you've been doing?'

'She was definitely getting suspicious about our meetings under the reading tree,' said Evie.

'Yes, she had all the branches of the tree chopped off so that we couldn't meet there any more,' Betsy pointed out.

Mouse rubbed his hands together nervously. His cheeks had gone red. 'I ... I ... I think it's my fault,' he said miserably. 'My Dream Map, the one about us meeting in the school...it went missing. I could have sworn I put it in my pocket, but I couldn't find it anywhere. I didn't say anything because I was so embarrassed. I have no idea how Miss Longbottom could have got hold of it, but that must be how she knew where we were going in our dreams that night. She was waiting for us.'

Mouse looked sheepishly at Jack. But Jack's mind was elsewhere. He had gone pale and he was staring at the book in his lap. 'That's not all she has,' he said.

Great Granny Georgia looked at him with raised eyebrows.

Jack swallowed before speaking. Then, so softly it was almost a whisper, he said: 'A couple of weeks ago my dream journal went missing.'

CHAPTER THIRTY

It had never occurred to Jack that someone might have stolen his dream journal. He had searched his bedroom high and low. Actually, he'd suspected the most likely cause of its disappearance was that his sister had taken it. He could imagine Bella reading it every night, arming herself with ammunition to make fun of him for years to come. But it had not crossed his mind that someone might have taken his journal to use against him — to interfere with his dreams.

'Your dream journal is the most powerful thing you can possess,' said Great Granny Georgia, shaking her head. 'It's very dangerous if it falls into the wrong hands. Think about it - it's a window into your deepest subconscious mind.'

Great Granny paused to survey her audience. Then she continued: 'If Miss Longbottom has one of your Dream Journals and one of your Dream Maps, she has a huge advantage over you. She has access to your inner selves. She knows your personal dream signs and she knows where you like to go. But most importantly, she knows where your nightmares take you. She knows your worst fears. And that's how people control others, through their fears.'

'I don't really understand,' said Betsy. 'How are people controlled through fear?'

'Well…. you all know what it's like to feel scared. Close your eyes for a moment and try to remember that feeling.'

The children did as Great Granny Georgia instructed and closed their eyes. They all tried to think of the last time they had felt afraid. Jack remembered when he had woken from a nightmare and was convinced he was still in it. He remembered how his heart had been pounding so fast that he thought his chest might burst. Mouse thought back to the nightmare when he had been naked in the school. Evie recalled the time she had lost sight of her parents for an hour while on holiday and couldn't speak enough Spanish to explain what had happened. Betsy couldn't think of anything for a little while. She didn't feel scared very often. Then it came back to her – the time her little sister had toppled into the pond. Her mum had screamed and waded in after her. It seemed an age before she dragged her out spluttering and gasping. Betsy had wanted to help, but she'd stood rooted to the spot, paralysed by fear.

'Are you all feeling it now?' Great Granny Georgia asked. 'Fear does something strange to people, you see. It makes them small and weak and powerless. It changes them into something they wouldn't normally be.'

'But everyone has fears.' said Jack. 'Everyone feels scared sometimes, don't they?'

'Yes they do. But it all depends on how you deal with those fears. Once you face up to your worst fears and refuse to back down, you emerge stronger. When you are no longer scared, you can achieve anything.'

Great Granny Georgia took a sip of tea while the children digested this information. 'This is what you must do. You must work out a way to overcome the evil force that has taken control of your dream realm. Dream worlds should not be places where nightmares can take root and make you afraid. They should be beautiful safe places where your imaginations can run wild and your greatest hopes and craziest thoughts can be realised. Somehow or other you must take back the reins.'

CHAPTER THIRTY-ONE

That evening the four of them sat in Jack's attic, mulling things over.

'It's Miss Longbottom's bird - I'm sure that's the key,' said Betsy. 'It has to be a vulture.' She began reading out loud from the book Great Granny Georgia had given them. *To see a vulture in your dream may indicate that someone is being opportunistic. They want to use you. They are watching you and waiting for you to make a mistake or show a weakness.'*

'So how do we fight back?' asked Evie. She took the book and flicked through the pages. 'Hey, listen to this. It says here that a dove is the antithesis of a vulture in dream worlds.'

'What does anti-the-sis mean?' asked Mouse.

'It means the exact opposite,' said Betsy impatiently. 'Go on, Evie.'

Evie read from the book: *The dove symbolizes peace, tranquility, hope, love and purity. It counteracts everything the vulture stands for. The dove is stronger than the vulture. It is the most powerful creature in the dream universe. Its presence can dispel any darkness or fears that may have infiltrated your dream world.'*

'This is all so confusing,' said Betsy. 'I mean, how do we get a dove into our dream world?'

'There must be something we can do,' said Evie

'Yes,' agreed Jack. 'It's important information. Information is knowledge and knowledge is power. It's the only way we're going to be able to take on Miss Longbottom.'

'There's only one thing for it,' said Mouse. 'We need to break into her office.'

'And do what?' asked Jack. 'Kill the vulture?'

'I'm not killing an animal,' said Betsy firmly. 'Not even a nightmare-spreading vulture.'

'Perhaps we could set it free,' suggested Mouse. 'Then maybe she couldn't use it anymore?'

'We don't know that for sure, though,' said Jack. 'It might become even more powerful if it's free.'

The children sat for a while, stumped for an answer. Eventually Jack spoke again: 'Well, let's see what we can find in her office anyway. It might give us some clues about what to do next.'

'But how on earth do we get into her office?' Mouse asked. 'There's no chance of doing it while everyone's at school. It would be far too dangerous. And we can't exactly break in at night, can we?'

'Wait,' said Evie, who had been sitting quietly for a while. 'I think I know how we can do it'.

The others looked at her expectantly.

'A month or two ago Miss Longbottom saw me pick up some conkers near the school gates. I was going to give them to my little brother - he loves playing conkers - but she accused me of planning to break a school window with them and said I had to be punished. She marched me inside and made me stand outside her office for three hours with my hands above my head.'

'And…? asked Betsy impatiently.

'Well the thing is,' went on Evie, 'she took me into the school through the back door - the one's that reserved for the teachers. It's the door can only be opened by using a keypad.'

'Yes, I've seen the keypad,' said Jack. 'It's so that us kids can't use that door. But how does this help us?'

'Well,' explained Evie, 'I remember noticing that Miss Longbottom entered a six-digit code to make the door open…'

Jack looked at her admiringly. 'A six-digit code. The number Mr Burley wrote on the blackboard . 5 – 9 – 2 – 3 – 9 – 4. You're a genius, Evie. That's got to be it. Mr Burley was telling us how to get into the school. It's like Great Granny Georgia said - *knowledge is power.*'

Chapter Thirty-Two

The next night the children arranged to sneak out of their bedrooms and meet at the school. For real, this time. Not in their dream world. They all agreed they had to get to the bottom of the mystery once and for all.

Jack rolled some clothes into a sausage shape and stuffed them under the duvet to make it look as if he was asleep in bed. He was pretty sure his mum wouldn't check up on him, but better safe than sorry. He could hear his sister talking in a low murmur in her bedroom, probably on the phone to a friend. Other than that, the house was still. Shadows flickered across the landing as he crept down the stairs, holding his breath as he clicked the door shut behind him. Grabbing his bike from the porch, he pedalled off down the road. When he arrived at the school gate, he found Betsy, Evie and Mouse waiting for him.

Jack paused and looked at the others solemnly. He felt he should say something, so he took a deep breath. 'Whatever we find in there … well, it could be big. We need to be careful. Right, let's go then.'

They crept round to the back of the school until they reached the door reserved for teachers. The keypad was on the wall beside it. Its monitor light shone red. Jack had brought the piece of paper with the number written on it, but he needn't have bothered as the sequence was imprinted on his memory. *5 – 9 – 2 – 3 – 9 – 4.*

'Well, here goes,' he said.

'Wait! What if there's an alarm?' asked Mouse.

'Well, we'll just have to take that risk. If it's the right code, we'll be okay. If it's not, and an alarm goes off - or anything else happens - just make a run for it. Right?'

'Okay, let's do it,' agreed Evie.

Mouse and Evie took a step backwards while Betsy shone a torch at the keypad so that Jack could see the numbers clearly in the dim light. He pressed each number firmly. *5 – 9 – 2 – 3 – 9 – 4*

As he pressed the final digit, there was a snap as something inside the door seemed to release and the light on the monitor turned green. The door swung slowly open.

Jack caught his breath. He could hardly believe it had actually worked. It proved beyond any doubt that they were able to transfer information from the dream realm to the real world, just like Dr Maria Dolores. He also knew there was no time to waste. 'Right, come on, quickly,' he urged the others. 'Remember what we're here for. No time to lose.' He led the way along the corridor and through the door into Miss Longbottom's office.

It took a while for his eyes to adjust to the darkness. Slowly the objects around him came into focus in the dim light. He saw Miss Longbottom's desk, piled high with books and papers. He saw the covered birdcage in the corner of the room.

Betsy walked over to the desk and began flicking through a big black notebook. She stared at the pages in fascination. Jack gazed across the room at the birdcage. He braced himself for what he knew he must do. He was about to go and remove its cover when he heard a noise somewhere down the corridor...a soft thud, like a footstep. He stood stock still. There it was again. Another footstep, only closer. Someone - or something - was walking slowly down corridor towards Miss Longbottom's office. Towards *them*.

CHAPTER THIRTY-THREE

The children looked at each other in horror.

'We need to get out of here.' hissed Betsy. 'We'll have to use the window.' She was still holding the black notebook and after a moment's hesitation she bundled it into her backpack. Another book on the desk caught her eye. It looked like a diary of some sort. She grabbed that too and stuffed it in with the notebook.

'What about the vulture?' whispered Evie. As if in response, there was a rasping hiss from inside the covered birdcage.

'There's no time for that,' said Betsy. 'We need to get out of here.' She ran to the window, lifted the latch and flung it open. First she, then Evie and Mouse, hoisted themselves on to the sill, climbed through the window and dropped down on to the path outside.

Jack was the last one left in the room. He looked at the covered birdcage, and as he did so he heard another footstep in the corridor. Whoever was out there had almost reached the door of Miss Longbottom's office. He ran towards the window, yanking the cover from the birdcage as he went.

He stopped and gasped. Staring out at him was a mighty bird. It was so huge that it filled the whole cage, and its jet-black feathers spilled out between the bars. Its gnarled beak was curved into what looked like a snarl. Its most striking detail was its piercing red eyes. They stared at him angrily and seemed to burn through his skin.

Jack felt as if he had been sent into a trance by the vulture's eyes. He snapped out of the spell and rushed the rest of the way to the window. As he climbed through it he took one last look round. The vulture was staring at him, its fiery eyes penetrating the darkness. And the handle of the door was beginning to turn.

Without waiting to see who or what came through the door, he dropped to the ground. The others were waiting for him and together they stumbled back along the path. Jack felt a prickling on the back of his neck and felt certain that someone or something was watching them. Just before he hurled himself through the gap in the hedge, he paused for second, trying to decide whether to turn around. He was scared of what he might see if he did, and decided he would rather not know. He followed the others through the hedge without looking back.

If Jack had turned around, he might have seen the black silhouette of Miss Longbottom staring after them from her office window and two flaming red eyes penetrating the darkness from the cage next to her.

CHAPTER THIRTY-FOUR

They each went back straight to their own houses. They were desperate to talk about what had happened, but felt it was too risky to do so right away. The last thing they needed was for their parents to become suspicious again.

The next day was Saturday. The Dream Squad agreed to meet at Jack's house that afternoon. There they pored over the black notebook that Betsy had grabbed from Miss Longbottom's office. It was old and tattered, and its pages were filled with creepy drawings and strange words.

'What ARE these?' murmured Mouse. As well as the pictures and words, there were initials on each page. The pictures were dark and shadowy. There were drawings of spiders and skeletons, monsters and graveyards.

Jack took the book and selected a page at random. It contained a drawing of a boy with a snake around his neck. The boy had his eyes shut and his mouth was pursed in terror. Jack turned to another page. It showed a sea of cockroaches swarming over a child asleep in bed. Another page showed an angry, shouting man. In one hand he held a bottle of beer, and with his other hand he was hurling a glass to the floor. Another showed a monster with dripping fangs and glowing eyes reaching through a window to pluck a child from its bed. Yet another depicted a boy swimming in the ocean. A shark was circling him, waiting for the right moment to make its move. Another showed a man throwing a child into the back of a van. The child was bound and gagged.

Realization began to dawn on Jack. He carried on turning the pages, engrossed by the pictures. One was of a little girl whose teeth had spilled out in front of her on to the floor. She was desperately trying to gather them up, but they just slipped through her fingers. A boy stood in the front of the school at assembly, shivering and ashamed while the pupils and teachers pointed and laughed. He was completely naked.

Jack turned to the last page. It showed a boy trapped in a box beneath the earth. He was scrabbling to get out of the tiny space, but the earth above him was too heavy. Jack put his fingers onto the drawing and traced them over the initials next to the picture. J.O.

'I know what this is,' he said. 'It's a collection of people's worst fears. It's a book of nightmares. And this last one…this one is mine.'

CHAPTER THIRTY-FIVE

Evie grabbed the book and thumbed through it. Now she saw it for herself… page after page of the darkest parts of people's imaginations. The parts that everyone keeps hidden, tucked away in the recesses of their minds. The things that no one ever talks about. The secrets that come out to haunt them in the dead of night, when there is nowhere else to hide.

She stopped at a page and stared at the picture in front of her. The colour drained from her face.

'What is it?' asked Jack.

She didn't answer, but passed the book to Jack so that he could see for himself. The picture was of a forest clearing. A child stood in the middle of the clearing surrounded by dark shadowy creatures. In the corner of the picture were the initials E.W.

Jack recognized the picture immediately. This wasn't any old clearing. This was the forest clearing they'd been in the other night when they were dreaming. 'This is your nightmare, isn't it?' he said. 'This is the one we shared with you.'

'Yes', said Evie. 'It's the same nightmare I've had since I was little. Whenever I'm worried or afraid, it comes back and I'm in that clearing.'

'But how does Miss Longbottom manage it?' asked Mouse. 'How can she know our deepest fears?'

Evie breathed in sharply. 'Wait. Do you remember the time she gave us all a writing assignment? We had to write an essay about something that frightened us. Maybe that was how she started collecting information about our fears.'

'Yes, I remember!' said Jack. 'And the more information she has about our fears, the more power she has to spread terror at night.'

'And she has the vulture, don't forget … the carrier of nightmares…' said Evie.

'But why *would* she?' asked Betsy. 'Why would she collect bad dreams to give us nightmares?'

'Who knows why people do bad things?' said Jack. 'Power, control, jealousy. It's like Great Granny Georgia said…once someone knows your darkest fears, they have a strange power over you. For whatever reason, she is behind all this, I just know it. Somehow she turned our dream in the forest into a nightmare. She tapped into your fears, Evie, and she did the same to you, Mouse, when you found yourself naked in school. She's trying to control us by making us experience our worst nightmares.'

'We need to figure out how she does it,' said Evie. 'It's the only way we can stop her.' She turned to Betsy. 'Didn't you take another book from Miss Longbottom's office?'

'Yes,' said Betsy. 'I haven't looked at it yet. I think it's a diary. Maybe it will give us some answers.'

She reached into her bag and passed the book to Jack, who began flicking through it. It was old, with faded handwriting and dog-eared pages. 'Yes,' he said, 'it does seem to be a journal. There's a different date on each page. And…wow, this first entry is from 1973. That means it's almost forty-five years old.'

'What does it say?' asked Mouse.

Jack began to read aloud from the book.

CHAPTER THIRTY-SIX

12th October 1973

Today O and W cornered me in the playground and called me names all lunchtime. The teachers did nothing to stop them. Neither did Alice, who is supposed to be my friend. After school I cried for an hour in my bedroom. I can't tell my mother what happened, as she will only say that I must have done something to irritate them.

17th October 1973

Today O stole my homework and tore it up. The teacher was angry and made me stand in the corner all morning. I couldn't say anything because W told me they would hurt me if I did.

25th October 1973

Today was one of the worst days so far. O and W taunted me all day. They cornered me at break time and told me that my father left home because I am horrid and ugly. They said my mother was useless and couldn't afford new clothes for me. Then they ripped my shirt and laughed because they knew I'd have to keep wearing it for the rest of term. I'm not sure I can take much more of this.

15th November 1973

The torment never ends. Why won't they leave me alone?

25th November 1973

Today they took my new jacket and threw it in the pond. Mother was furious with me. She asked me how I could be so thoughtless when I knew how little money we had.

28th November 1973

I have no friends, there is no one at all. Nobody cares about me. I'm so miserable.

14th December 1973

Today, O and W cut both my plaits off with a pair of scissors. They were sitting behind me in class and the teacher didn't see. Now I look like a scruffy boy. The whole class laughed at me. I cried myself to sleep.

18th December 1973

Normally I would be excited about Christmas, but I feel no joy this year. O and W flushed my face in the toilet at school and I am not going in tomorrow. I made myself vomit so that mother wouldn't make me go.

10th January 1974

A new year and nothing has changed. Back to school today and the teasing and torment continued. The teachers don't care and my mother doesn't believe me. No one knows how bad it is.

16th January 1974

How can children be so cruel? I don't understand it. From now on, I will look out only for myself. One day, I will be older and will get my revenge. That's what keeps me going. The thought of getting my revenge on all children.

CHAPTER THIRTY-SEVEN

There was a long silence. 'Poor Miss Longbottom. I almost feel sorry for her,' said Mouse.

'I find it impossible to imagine her as a little girl,' said Evie. 'I've always felt she must have been born a nasty old woman!'

'I know what you mean,' said Jack. 'It's hard to think of her being bullied.'

'I guess we know now why she's the way she is,' said Mouse.

Jack nodded. 'She's obviously decided that children are evil.'

'It's like she decided to take revenge on all children,' said Mouse. 'That must have been why she became a head teacher.'

'It seems a bit extreme,' said Jack. 'She was only being bullied by two children.'

'Well…being bullied is terrible,' said Mouse. 'I've been teased a few times and it's the worst. But this bullying she writes about in her diary… well it sounds so horrible, and it went on for such a long time. It must have changed her, and made angry with the world.'

'So she made a vow to gain power over children and destroy their lives,' said Betsy.

'That makes sense,' said Evie. 'I've always wondered why someone who hates children so much would become a head teacher.'

Jack was distracted. He was flicking through the big black notebook again. 'I'm sure I saw it… where is it…yes, here!' It was the last picture in the book. It was smaller than the rest and only covered a quarter of the page. It was a sketch of a little girl. She was sitting at a desk with her head in her hands. Tears were rolling down her cheeks. Two bigger children loomed over her. Their fists were raised.

'It's her nightmare,' said Jack. 'Her own worst fear.'

The initials next to the picture were V.L.

Vera Longbottom.

Chapter Thirty-Eight

J ack spoke with a confidence that he wasn't feeling. 'Right. Is everyone clear on what we're doing?'

They all nodded. How could they not be? They'd gone over it a dozen times.

'Shall we go through it one final time?' asked Evie, trying to hide her nervousness.

Betsy rolled her eyes, but Jack nodded patiently. 'Of course we can. Right. First, I will burn the book. That way, we destroy Miss Longbottom's record of everyone's fears. That will reduce her power. Then we all go into the nightmare realm together to find her and destroy her vulture by visualising the doves.'

'Hmm, sounds so simple,' Betsy muttered.

Jack ignored her. 'Most importantly, we must not be afraid. We can overcome the nightmare if we show no fear. Whatever happens, we must stay strong and face up to it. We must keep reminding ourselves that it is all in our minds That way, she will have nothing over us.'

The others nodded solemnly.

Mouse had been half-listening and half-flicking through the book that Great Granny Georgia had given them. 'Listen to this,' he said. 'This chapter talks about the dream herbs we've tried, the ones that can bring on lucid dreaming. But it also talks about herbs that should be avoided – herbs and teas that can tap into a different part of the dream world and can cause nightmares and night terrors.'

Evie shivered. 'Why would anyone want to take *them*?'

'Well, that's the point. I think we *should* take them. We have to enter willingly into the nightmare realm to find Miss Longbottom and her vulture. If we are reluctant or afraid, she'll sense our fear.'

Jack nodded, a little hesitantly. 'You're right. Rather than be frightened of the nightmare, we need to go in bravely and be ready to conquer it.'

Evie grimaced. 'I still can't believe we are going to enter a nightmare on purpose.'

Jack tried to sound reassuring. 'Just remember — she can't hurt us. Only our fears can.'

After the others had left, Jack placed Miss Longbottom's book of nightmares on the ground outside the shed and reached in his pocket for the box of matches he'd taken from the kitchen. He struck a match and held it to the pages. As the flames grew stronger and starting to envelop the book, they seemed to shudder and turn black. Alarmed, Jack stepped backwards. There was a strange squealing sound and the flames grew blacker and fiercer. Images seemed to leap out of the book…terrifying black figures, dancing and writhing, silhouetted against the orange flames. The squealing became louder until it was almost unbearable. In the centre of the fire was a black figure. It was trying desperately to scrabble out of a hole in the ground…it was his own nightmare emerging from the flames in front of his very eyes.

Jack rubbed his eyes and looked again. The flames were still black but the figures had disappeared and the squealing had stopped. Had he imagined it? Another minute passed and the flames subsided. The book had been reduced to ashes. Jack stamped on them. Satisfied that the book was completely destroyed he went back to the house.

CHAPTER THIRTY-NINE

That night, everyone felt nervous. Jack was restless. He barely heard his mum nagging him about his homework, which made her moan even more. He picked at his dinner and pushed it around the plate with his fork, pretending to eat a spoonful here and there. His stomach was in knots.

He was in his bedroom by 7pm, which was a record even for him. His mum had stopped complaining and seemed a little concerned. She tapped softly at his door.

'Jack?' she whispered. 'Is everything okay?'

'I'm fine, Mum.' He snapped without meaning to. He couldn't deal with his mum interrupting him tonight.

His mum pushed open the door an inch and peered through the gap. 'You've been so quiet this afternoon. And you hardly touched your dinner. Has something happened at school?'

'No Mum, I'm just tired, that's all.'

'Right. Well…' For once in her life his mum was almost lost for words. 'Well… you know I only nag because I care, don't you Jack?'

'Sure, Mum.'

It was strange. It was almost as though she sensed something important was about to happen. 'Right, well get a good night's sleep then.'

'Yes, Mum. Goodnight.'

She closed the door, and Jack felt his stomach clench again. He lay back on his bed, staring at the ceiling. 'Face your fears,' he repeated over and over to himself. He tried to imagine what his Great Granny Georgia would say to him now. He closed his eyes and pictured her kind, wrinkled old face as she tucked him into his bed and kissed his forehead with her puckered lips. 'Just remember, Jack. The dream world is magical. It can't hurt you. It is only your fears that hurt you. So it's simple Jack, just don't be afraid.'

Jack sat up and reached under his bed for a pencil and a notebook. He tore a sheet from the notebook and scribbled some words on it. Then he slipped the piece of paper under his pillow, lay back down again and closed his eyes.

The words on the paper said: *Dear Mum, Dad and Bella. If I stay asleep it's because I'm stuck in a dream … please try everything you can to wake me up. Don't give up on me. (I'm sorry).*

CHAPTER FORTY

J ack stepped into a bleak landscape. He sensed immediately that this was not a safe place. It felt different to the dream world with which he was familiar.

He looked around. The land was desolate and grey. The only signs of life were huge birds of prey that were feeding off unidentifiable carcasses. One stared at him for a second with piercing red eyes and emitted a low, raspy squawk that seemed to be a warning of some type. Then it went back to pecking the remains in front of it.

Jack shivered, and kept repeating to himself: 'I'm dreaming, I'm safe. Don't be afraid. I'm dreaming, I'm safe.'

The sun blasted down, strong on the back of his neck. He felt dizzy from the heat. He strained his eyes, looking for any of the others, but all he could see, stretching to the horizon, were the birds and the carcasses on which they were feeding.

'Come on, you lot,' he muttered, trying to visualize them in front of him. No one appeared. Perhaps things were harder to conjure up in this nightmare world. Everything felt different. There seemed to be a force of resistance working against him.

He heard a hiss and saw a large snake slithering across the desert towards him. Its scales glistened as it slid closer. He felt a knot of fear in the pit of his stomach. The knot travelled up towards his throat but no sound came out. He was terrified of snakes. He fought off the urge to run away or to try and wake himself up. 'It can't hurt me. It's just a dream. It can't hurt me.'

His mouth was dry. He blinked hard, and when he opened his eyes again the snake was gone.

A huge shadow passed across the sun, darkening the sky. Despite the heat, Jack shivered. He heard a loud rasping noise and the flap of a huge wing. He scanned the horizon, starting to feel panic rising up inside him.

Where were the others? What was he going to do if he couldn't find them? How could he fight the vulture alone?

CHAPTER FORTY-ONE

J ack started to trudge across the desolate land. Every step was a tremendous effort even though the ground was flat. His energy seemed to be draining from him. He didn't seem to be making any progress. He felt as if he was in one of those computer games where you just go on and on and never seem to get anywhere.

He kept trying to visualize the others. Usually when he did this, it wasn't long before they appeared. But not this time. It felt like a different type of dream, a dark, sinister dream where everything was that much harder.

It became harder and harder to walk. He paused and looked around. In an instant, the ground seemed to melt away and he found himself stranded on a tiny piece of land, surrounded by black swampy waters. In the water he could see writhing scaly bodies and flashes of white teeth.

'This is a dream, I'm safe, they can't hurt me,' he muttered, but he was finding it hard to quell his rising fear.

What if he became trapped here like Mr Burley or Eliza, on his own, forever? What if no one could wake him up? What if he were stranded on this tiny island, surrounded by evil creatures for the rest of time? He started to pinch himself, but to his alarm, nothing happened.

He heard a rasping squawk and a huge black bird, with wings wider than his out-stretched arms, swooped down and landed in front of him. It hissed at him, its sharp, jagged beak inches from his face, its red eyes like two burning coals. Jack took a step backwards and felt the sand beneath his feet begin to crumble and give way. He was sliding closer and closer to the thrashing, squirming waters.

As he dropped deeper into the nightmare and felt himself falling towards the snapping jaws in the water beneath him, a hand reached out and pulled him up onto the vulture's back.

CHAPTER FORTY-TWO

'**M**r Burley!' Jack gasped.

'Jack'.

Jack found himself sitting with Mr Burley on the vulture's back. The sand was still crumbling away, and the creatures were writhing in the swampy water.

Mr Burley looked weary and miserable. 'What are you doing here, Jack?'

'We've come to rescue you! And to get rid of Miss Longbottom and her nightmares once and for all.'

Mr Burley shook his head sadly. 'I don't think she can be stopped.'

'Of course she can. We've got to try.'

'She's become so powerful in the dream world, you see. She causes almost all of the nightmares people have. With me, she went further. She wanted to get rid of me altogether.'

'But why Mr Burley? Why you?'

'She hated me for being kind to you kids. Most of the teachers were too scared to stand up to her, but I couldn't bear to see you suffer so much. I was getting in the way of her plan to make all children miserable.'

'Did you realise what she was up to?'

'Well, not the full extent of it but I was becoming suspicious. One day I had gone to her office to confront her about a detention she had given the whole school. The door was slightly ajar, so I poked my head in and I noticed this bulky notebook on her desk. I was intrigued so I walked over and opened it. I wasn't sure what it all meant, but *it was pretty clear that she had been collecting children's nightmares. Then I heard a hiss, and at that moment Miss Longbottom stormed in and caught me with the book. Her face contorted with rage, but instead of firing me as I expected, she didn't say a word. A few days later, the nightmares started.'*

He added dryly: 'I suppose she thought it would be easier if I could disappear in the dream world rather than the real world — less chance of me suing her for unfair dismissal.'

'How did she do it? How did she trap you?'

'She discovered my greatest fear... growing old alone. She used this fear to take over my dreams and turn them into nightmares. In every dream I had for weeks, I found myself old and desperately lonely. I'd wake up in a cold sweat. I started to become so frightened of dreaming that I avoided sleep as much as I could. But that didn't help at all, of course. I just became more tired and frail and the nightmares got worse. One night, when I was weak from fear and exhaustion, she used the vulture to trap me in a dream...and I've been stuck here ever since.'

He paused. 'Tell me, what are people saying has happened to me?'

'Miss Longbottom has told everyone at school that you're unwell.'

Mr Burley stared into the distance, looking sad. 'How's everyone getting on with their chemistry?'

Jack smiled. 'Don't worry, Mr Burley, everyone has been keeping up. In fact, Miss Longbottom has been working us VERY hard. But she doesn't let us do any fun experiments like you do. She just makes us copy out page after page of our textbooks. Everyone wants you to come back. School is unbearable without you there. We have to figure out a way to get you out of...'

Before he could finish his sentence there was a loud hissing noise and the vulture they were sitting on beat its huge wings and lifted into the sky.

CHAPTER FORTY-THREE

J ack felt helpless as the bird carried them through the air. Usually he could
visualise things in his dreams and make them happen, but not this time. It
was as though his mind had gone blank and he was completely powerless. He
looked at Mr Burley, clinging on next to him, and saw the same hopelessness in his
face.

The bird's wings flapped noisily and a rasping sound came from its beak. The sky
became dark and Jack could no longer see anything at all. He closed his eyes, ready
to give up.

He felt a sudden falling sensation. He realised that he had slipped off the
vulture's back and was plummeting through the air. 'Just a dream, just a dream,' he
kept telling himself.

With a sudden jolt, he found himself in a dark cave. He waited for his eyes to
adjust to the darkness, but they didn't. 'Mr Burley?'

He heard a grunt next to him and Mr Burley muttered something. He seemed to
be fumbling for his glasses.

Suddenly there was another voice. Jack felt a surge of happiness. 'Mouse!'

'Jack. Jack! JACK!'

Jack wondered why Mouse kept repeating his name. 'I'm right here, Mouse, right
here,' he mumbled.

'Jack, Jack!'

Jack was becoming irritated. Why wouldn't Mouse stop saying his name? He
started drifting out of the cave and realised it wasn't Mouse calling his name any
more. It was his mum and she was standing over him calling his name to wake him up.

CHAPTER FORTY-FOUR

'No!' Jack sat upright in his bed. 'No, I need to stay asleep!'

'Um, no actually, Jack – you NEED to get up for school, right now - or you're going to be late. Did you forget to set your alarm?' Without waiting for an answer she stalked out of his room. Any concern she had shown last night had evaporated.

Jack lay there, his heart thumping, thinking about Mr Burley and Mouse. He felt he had been about to get somewhere but had woken up too soon. He and the others would have to try again tonight.

He was about to leave for school when the phone rang. It was unusual for someone to call that early. He half listened as his mum pick up the receiver.

'Oh! Hello! Is everything okay? You're sure? Oh, Jack? Right…was it something in particular? Um, okay, of course. I'll get him… JACK!'

Jack headed back into the kitchen, wondering who on earth could be wanting to speak to him.

'It's … it's your Great Granny Georgia on the phone,' said his mum.

He grabbed the phone. 'Great-Granny?'

Jack could see his mum loitering nearby, pretending to clear up the kitchen table, desperate to know what Great Granny Georgia wanted. He lowered his voice as much as he could. 'What is it?'

'Jack. I need you to listen carefully. I've remembered something that might help you conquer the dream world… Remember I told you about Dr Maria Dolores?'

CHAPTER FORTY-FIVE

J ack hurried to school, eager to talk to the others. It was only yesterday since he had last seen them, but it seemed like a lifetime.

Miss Longbottom had put the whole class in detention during both the morning and lunch breaks (she had said their pencils weren't sharp enough) and it wasn't until the bell rang for the end of school that the four of them were able to talk.

Jack spoke first. 'I was with Mr Burley last night. What happened? Where were you all?'

'I saw you just before I woke up,' said Mouse. 'You were in my cave.'

'What do you mean, *your* cave?'

'I was stuck in this cave for what felt like forever,' said Mouse. 'It was horrible. I couldn't find a way out, no matter how hard I tried. It was like my mind went blank. I couldn't seem to remember anything. At the end of the nightmare, just before I woke up, I heard you calling my name, but I couldn't get to you.'

'What about you guys?' Jack turned to Betsy and Evie.

'I was stuck in my nightmare too.' said Evie. 'It was terrifying. I was in the clearing I'm always in. The shadows and the creatures were closing in on me. This time it seemed to go on forever and there was no escape.'

'I felt trapped too,' said Betsy. 'I was in a dark room. I think it was a cellar. It was horrid. I kept trying to find you all, but I couldn't.'

'Miss Longbottom still has great power over us,' said Jack. 'She can still trap us in our nightmares. Listen, Great Granny Georgia phoned me this morning. She reminded me that when you're in a nightmare, the fear clouds your senses. You are scared, so you are less in control. All you feel is overwhelming fear. That's why we couldn't find each other and we couldn't remember what to do.'

The others nodded in agreement. They knew that feeling.

'Remember the research that Dr Maria Dolores did on anchor objects and how she used to draw a little picture on her hand?' Jack went on. 'The drawings would help guide her to complete her task and locate her anchor object in the dream world. Great Granny Georgia suggested that we try this technique. We could all draw doves on our hands, which will help to unite us in the dream and focus us on our mission'.

CHAPTER FORTY-SIX

That night, all four went to bed earlier than usual again. Evie, who was the best artist, had drawn a dove on each of their hands to help unite them and focus them on their mission.

As Jack returned to his nightmare, he tried to stay strong. All they had to do was remember not to be afraid of the dark. To face their fears and unite in the dream.

And now they had a focal point, a reminder of what they needed to do.

He felt himself drifting off to sleep and instantly he found himself back in the cave with Mr Burley. Mouse was there too. It was as though his dream was continuing exactly where he had left off.

Mr Burley's hands and feet were tied with rope and he was lying on the floor of the cave with his eyes closed. Jack tried to untie the ropes, but the more he tried, the tighter they became. It felt like those magic birthday candles that kept coming alight no matter how many times you blew them out.

A shard of light from somewhere shone across Jack's hand and illuminated the picture of the dove. He paused and looked up to see where the light was coming from. Then he turned to Mouse, who was crouching next to him. 'Mouse, let's get the girls here. I think I can see an opening in the corner of the cave.'

Mouse looked up. It was true. There was sunlight coming through it. They walked towards it and peered through the narrow gap. 'Visualise Evie and Betsy on the other side,' Jack whispered.

To their horror the crack started to break apart. Shards of rock flew everywhere. Stones began falling on them until they were nearly buried in rubble. Jack was finding *it hard to breathe. He looked at the dove on his hand and remembered Great Granny Georgia's words – 'Show No Fear'. He realised that this was his worst nightmare – being buried alive, trapped until he couldn't breathe. But he had to show he wasn't afraid. It was only a dream. IT WAS ONLY A DREAM.*

He said the words over and over again, and as he did so the rocks started to crumble away and he found he could breathe again. He looked up and saw Evie. She was in a dark clearing. Creatures lurked all around her.

'It's your nightmare Evie!' he yelled, but his words seemed to be whisked away on the wind. 'It's your worst fear – try not to be afraid!'

He saw Evie stare at the dove on her hand. She looked up and locked eyes with Jack. There was a look of determination on her face. The clearing brightened and the creatures around her faded away.

Betsy was grappling with a snake that had wrapped itself around her. 'Stay strong Betsy! It can't hurt you if you're not afraid.' She looked at her hand and the snake slithered away.

Mouse was cowering in a corner of the cave with no clothes on. His hands covered his ears, trying to block out the mocking laughter echoing round the cave.

'Mouse, it's not real!' Jack yelled. 'Remember, it's a nightmare, nothing more.' He held his hand up so that Mouse could see the dove. Mouse unblocked his ears and looked down at his own hand. The sniggering laughter faded away and the cave became silent.

The four of them looked at each other, waiting in suspense, wondering what would happen next.

A thunderous crash filled the cave and a giant vulture lifted into the air with Miss Longbottom riding on the top of it. She gazed down at them, her face warped with rage. Without warning, the fury on her face turned to fear. The vulture vanished and she was enveloped in swathes of black smoke. Two giant children towered over her in the smoke, cackling and hissing. Jack realised who they were. They were the bullies from Miss Longbottom's own nightmare.

Miss Longbottom seemed to shrivel and shrink. She was turning into a helpless little girl. There was panic in her eyes.

Jack yelled out. 'You have to face your fears, Miss Longbottom! Show them you're not afraid. They don't have power over you any longer. They can't hurt you!'

Miss Longbottom looked over at Jack for a second. He wasn't sure but he thought there were tears on her face. The smoke was spreading fast and making Jack's eyes water. He put his hand up to wipe the tears from his face and once again caught he a glimpse of the drawing on his hand again. It jolted his memory and he shouted to the others. 'The doves – now!'

Together they focused their thoughts. A flock of doves, wings beating, rose into the air. As they did so, the black smoke drifted away, and Miss Longbottom and the bullies disappeared. Jack thought he could hear a vulture's rasping squawk somewhere far away, fading into the distance.

At that moment, he woke up.

His heart was pounding.

They had done it. They had faced their fears and escaped from their nightmares. Hadn't they?

CHAPTER FORTY-SEVEN

As they arrived at St Bartholomew's the next morning, the Dream Squad sensed something was different. It was as though the tension had lifted. The air itself felt lighter.

The first thing they did was head for the chemistry lab. Jack led the way and was the first to peer through the door.

He felt a surge of joy. Mr Burley was in there, setting up his Bunsen burners on the desks. He tested one of the burners and nearly torched his eyebrows. Jack smiled. Everything seemed back to normal there then.

Mr Burley looked up and saw Jack. He gave a half-smile and winked. Jack smiled back.

Jack turned to the others 'He's back! Now we need to find out what happened to Miss Longbottom.'

They headed towards Miss Longbottom's office. For the first time ever, the office door was wide open and they could see inside. The curtains were drawn and sunshine was spilling into the room. It was amazing how different the room looked. Miss Longbottom was nowhere to be seen, and the birdcage in the corner of her room was no longer covered. Not only that, it was empty too.

Jack heard a noise by the open window. Perched on the top of the window ledge was a dove. It was pure white and its feathers seemed to glimmer in the light. It was making a soft cooing noise and it cocked its head at Jack momentarily.

'Wow,' he murmured softly, but by the time the others had followed his gaze, there was nothing but an empty windowsill and the faint flutter of wings against the soft breeze.

CHAPTER FORTY-EIGHT

With no sign of Miss Longbottom in her office, the Dream Squad headed to the school hall and waited to see if she would appear. She was due to take assembly that morning, as she did every Friday. But suppose she hadn't woken up? Suppose she was still trapped in her nightmare?

The hands of the clock ticked round slowly to half past nine. Still no Miss Longbottom. Usually there was a hush in the hall before her arrival. Everyone was afraid of being caught talking. But today was different. Children began whispering and chatting to each other to pass the time.

Jack caught Betsy's eye. He raised his eyebrows slightly and knew she was thinking the same. Was Miss Longbottom gone for good? Had they consigned her to the dream world?

Tick tock, tick tock, tick tock. By 9.40 the other teachers in the hall were looking at each other questioningly, wondering to do.

And then she appeared.

It was hard to say exactly what was different about her but, yes, she had undoubtedly changed. She hesitated for a moment at the door. It was the first time the children had seen her look uncertain before. Not only that. Her face seemed to have softened. The hard wrinkles had smoothed out and her scowl had gone.

Jack let out a long breath. He felt relieved. Despite all the terrible things she had done over the years, he was pleased that she was not stuck in her nightmare, a little girl being bullied and tormented forever.

Although only five people in the hall (and one in the chemistry laboratory) knew the truth of what had happened, everyone sensed the change in Miss Longbottom. They weren't sure how she was different. They just knew there was nothing to be afraid of any more. Where previously a frightened silence would have descended on the hall, now there was now a low murmur as the children whispered to each other in amazement. Even the teachers seemed puzzled.

Miss Longbottom surveyed the children in the hall with a slightly confused look on her face. Then something extraordinary happened, causing everyone to gasp in astonishment.

For the first time since she was a little girl, Vera Longbottom smiled.

CHAPTER FORTY-NINE

The Dream Squad rushed to the reading tree as soon as the bell rang for morning break. Even though the tree was still limbless, it felt like the right place to meet.

'Well, I guess we did it,' smiled Evie.

'We sure did,' agreed Betsy.

Mouse nodded. 'No more nightmares!'

'Isn't it amazing how different everyone seems?' said Evie. 'Miss Longbottom has changed the most, of course - but have you noticed the change in everyone else too? Everyone seems so full of energy and so cheerful. Who knows how many others were losing sleep and walking around exhausted because of the nightmares they were having?'

'Yes, I've noticed that too,' said Mouse. 'It sort of feels as though a weight has been lifted off the whole school.'

Jack looked at each of his fellow adventurers in turn as they crouched under the stubby branches of the weeping willow. Already a few leaves were growing back, and the sun was shining through them, casting shadowy patterns on their faces. He felt proud to know them. Evie, Betsy and Mouse had become his closest friends over the past few months.

'I can't believe everything that's happened to us,' said Betsy.

'I know,' agreed Evie. 'It's just a shame we'll all be starting at different secondary schools after the summer holidays, and won't be seeing so much of each other.'

Jack smiled. 'Want a bet?"

The End

Printed in Great Britain
by Amazon